STARGAZER LILIES OR NOTHING AT ALL

STEPHEN LOMER

www.stephenlomer.com

ISBN: **1540519716**
ISBN-13: **978-1540519719**

DEDICATION

To all of my fellow authors, for helping me
believe that I could do it too.

ALSO AVAILABLE
BY STEPHEN LOMER

Typo Squad

CONTENTS

ACKNOWLEDGMENTS

Foremost, I must convey my eternal gratitude to my two partners in crime, Christopher Valin and Chris Whigham, who were always there to offer advice, recommend edits, and keep my literary compass pointed in the right direction. Special thanks to all the wonderfully talented authors I've met on this journey. And a very special thank you to my wife, Teresa, for all her love and support.

I. STARGAZER LILIES OR NOTHING AT ALL

Ermengarde was told at last to open her eyes, and when she finally did so, the very breath in her lungs was knocked away, as though she had taken an unexpectedly nasty tumble off her thoroughbred, Zeus.

The function hall at HillCleft Manor had been magically transformed into a wonderland befitting a woman of her station and the guests she'd invited. Candles, bunting, crepe, crystal, and every manner of finery one could conceive of had been combined in the most elegant way imaginable.

The predominant color was a robin's-egg blue, for Ermengarde had been informed some time ago that her forthcoming child would be a boy. Oh, if only little Pip could arrive sooner, and see the magnificent baby shower in which his mother was about to partake!

Ermengarde turned to her mother, both of them smiling broadly, and kissed the air around the older woman's cheek, left and right.

"Well, darling?" her mother asked. "Are you pleased?"

"Oh Mother, words fail me," Ermengarde gushed. "It is everything I ever could've hoped for."

"Excellent, my angel," her mother said. "It would be unacceptable to welcome my first grandson in a manner any less grand than this."

"Oh, I agree, Mother," Ermengarde said. "Wholeheartedly."

"Why don't you have a look around while I pop down to catering and ensure that everything there is as perfect as it is here?" her mother said.

"Very well, Mother," Ermengarde said. "But don't dally. The guests will be arriving straightaway."

"Five minutes," her mother said as she made her way to a side door nearby.

Ermengarde walked among the small tables that had been set around the room, admiring the gleam of the silverware and the sheen of the glasses. She passed the sturdy oak table that had been set aside to hold the innumerable gifts that were no doubt on their way. She stepped up on the carpeted platform where she'd be sitting on the velvet-lined throne as her baby shower commenced, and looked out and imagined all the faces of her friends and family as they gazed upon her lovingly.

A smartly dressed woman entered the room, carrying a massive bouquet of lilies that she placed on a plinth to the left of the throne. She left, then returned and placed another one to the right. Ermengarde stared at the lilies, suddenly and positively aghast.

"Oh, hello," the woman said, noticing Ermengarde on her

second trip into the room. "You must be the guest of honor."

"I am," Ermengarde said, unable to tear her now-bulging eyes away from the newly arrived arrangements.

The other woman extended her hand. "Miss Eleanor Sterling-Poundsworth, celebrity botanist."

"Ah," Ermengarde said, shaking the woman's hand lightly. "So would it be to you that I would direct my complaint? Or do you have underlings to handle that sort of thing?"

Eleanor frowned ever so slightly. "Complaint? I'm certain I don't know what you mean."

"These," Ermengarde said, pointing at the lilies that Eleanor had just brought in. "These are, I believe, tiger lilies, are they not?"

"Why yes they are," Eleanor replied. "They are, in fact, the finest tiger lilies in all of London. If I do say so myself."

"Ah," Ermengarde said. "Yes. That's as may be, but I'm dreadfully sorry to inform you that I don't care at all for tiger lilies."

"I see," Eleanor said. "Well then it's intensely curious that you would request tiger lilies for such a special occasion then, wouldn't you say?"

"It would be indeed, had I requested tiger lilies," Ermengarde said. "But as a point of fact, I specifically requested stargazer lilies."

"Did you?" Eleanor said, raising her eyebrows. "Permit me a moment to check my paperwork, won't you?"

"But of course," Ermengarde said.

Eleanor pulled an iPad from her handbag and tapped and swiped her way through a few screens. After a few moments she nodded.

"Yes, here it is, two large sprays of tiger lilies, ordered on the twelfth of last month."

"Oh heavens," Ermengarde said. "What a terrible shame that you misunderstood the order that was placed."

"I am one of the preeminent botanists in all of Britain, and I receive and handle every order myself," Eleanor said. "So I can assure you that if I have brought you tiger lilies, it is only because an order for tiger lilies was placed. Did you order them personally?"

"No," Ermengarde said. "My mummy ordered them."

"Ah," Eleanor said. "Then perhaps the error lies with her." Just then, Ermengarde's mother re-entered the room, scanning every detail.

"Mummy," Ermengarde said. "Are you attempting to ruin my life?"

"I'm sorry, darling?"

"This is Miss Eleanor Sterling-Poundsworth, celebrity botanist," Ermengarde said. Her mother crossed the room and took both of Eleanor's hands in hers.

"Oh, how delightful to meet you. The flowers are breathtaking."

"Oh, why thank you," Eleanor said.

"Mummy," Ermengarde continued, crossing her arms over the arch of her belly. "Miss Eleanor Sterling-Poundsworth claims that when ordering these particular bouquets, you chose tiger lilies. Is that true?"

"Why yes, darling," her mother said, admiring the arrangements. "Aren't they gorgeous?"

"Mummy," Ermengarde said. "Are you and I acquainted?"

Her mother smiled. "Well I should hope so. I've known

you since you were born, after all." She gave a small titter.

"Well then what I find impossible to fathom is how you could believe for the briefest of moments that I would accept tiger lilies instead of stargazer lilies."

Her mother considered her carefully. "My dear," she said at last, soothingly, "lilies are lilies."

"*Are* they?" Ermengarde said, her voice rising slightly. "Well, isn't it most fortunate for us that we have one the preeminent botanists in all of Britain in our midst. Tell me, Miss Eleanor Sterling-Poundsworth, is that an accurate statement? Are lilies lilies?"

"Well—" Eleanor began.

"No, lilies are *not* lilies, Mummy," Ermengarde said. "And while every other detail of this room is admittedly flawless, I cannot in good conscience overlook the fact that we are currently burdened with the incorrect lilies."

"Very well, my dear," her mother sighed. She turned to Eleanor. "Would it be at all possible to replace these lilies with the proper ones?"

"Oh indeed, certainly possible," Eleanor said. "Unfortunately, I fear, not in time for the baby shower."

"I see," her mother said.

"Well then, there's only one thing for it," Ermengarde said. She stepped as daintily off the platform as her delicate condition allowed and crossed to the grand entranceway. A few moments later, a sharply dressed footman stepped into the room.

"Dame Elizabeth Marie-Sistine Lovenbotham, and her daughter, Lady Freya Persephone Lovenbotham," the footman announced, and retreated. An older woman dressed in impeccable fashion and a younger woman similarly attired approached the entry, where Ermengarde met them.

"Dame Lovenbotham," Ermengarde said, kissing the air near both of the older woman's cheeks. "Lady Lovenbotham. So extraordinary to see you on this most glorious of days. It pains me to no end to be the bearer of such dreadful news, but I'm afraid the baby shower has been canceled."

"Oh my dear," Dame Lovenbotham said, a look of deep concern on her face. "Nothing untoward has happened to the child, has it?"

"Oh no, nothing of the kind," Ermengarde replied. "No, no. Something far more horrific. We have the improper lilies for the occasion."

"I beg your pardon?" Dame Lovenbotham said. "Did you say improper lilies?"

"Yes," Ermengarde said. "Tiger lilies in place of stargazer lilies. Can you even *imagine*?"

Dame Lovenbotham and her daughter stared blankly.

"Still, awfully kind of you to attend," Ermengarde continued. "I shall ensure your names are at the very top of the list when we send out invitations for the christening."

"My dear," Dame Lovenbotham said, "we came all the way from Cardiff."

"Yes, I know, quite a long trip, isn't it? Do have a safe journey back. And give my love to Lord Lovenbotham."

"Are you honestly canceling the festivities because of *lilies*?" Lady Lovenbotham asked.

Ermengarde looked at the young lady as if she'd gone utterly mad. "Well what would *you* do?"

Dame and Lady Lovenbotham considered this for a few

moments, and then both nodded their heads. "Yes, of course you're right, my dear," Dame Lovenbotham said, smiling.

"Whatever would you tell your son if you allowed this to go forward with things in such a *state?*" Lady Lovenbotham agreed.

"Oh, thank you both for understanding," Ermengarde said.

"Certainly, dear," Dame Lovenbotham said. She turned to her daughter. "Come, darling. If we leave now we might still make tea at The Montague."

"Farewell!" Ermengarde called as the two women left. She raised her hand to attract the attention of the footman, who hurried over.

"Yes, m'lady?"

"Would you be so kind as to inform the remaining guests who arrive that the shower has been canceled?" she said.

"Very good, m'lady," the footman bowed. "Shall I provide them a reason, if asked?"

"Yes," Ermengarde said. "Lilies."

"Very good, m'lady," the footman said, and disappeared. Ermengarde crossed the room to rejoin her mother and Eleanor.

"Well that's a disaster narrowly averted, Mummy," she said. "And more's the pity, too. Everything else was absolutely perfect."

"Yes," said her mother through pursed lips. "Indeed it was. You do realize, my darling, that a considerable expenditure of time, money, and effort went into this undertaking?"

"I do," said Ermengarde. "And how dreadful that one silly

mistake on your part has rent it all asunder."

Her mother's eyes narrowed, but Ermengarde had turned her attention to the celebrity botanist still in their midst. "Miss Eleanor Sterling-Poundsworth, as you are still here, might I make a request of you?"

"Why certainly," Eleanor said.

"In a fortnight, I shall find myself in the private maternity unit of The Kensington Wing at Chelsea and Westminster Hospital. Could you see to it that the private maternity unit of The Kensington Wing at Chelsea and Westminster Hospital is filled to capacity with *stargazer* lilies?"

Eleanor made some notes on her iPad. "Consider it done."

"Smashing," Ermengarde said with a smile. "And if, by some unforeseen circumstance, some *other* type of lily should be delivered to the private maternity unit of The Kensington Wing at Chelsea and Westminster Hospital, could you please ensure that stargazer lilies are sent to my padded cell at Nightingale Mental Hospital, as that will be where I spend the remainder of my days."

Ermengarde turned and began walking toward the exit. "Come, Mummy," she said, and her mother fell in step with her.

As they crossed the solarium beyond the function room, Ermengarde said, "Oh, how I envy you, Mummy."

"Oh?" her mother said. "And why would that be?"

"Well, it isn't every day that one learns such a valuable lesson, is it?"

Her mother nodded. "Oh, I learned quite the lesson today, dear," she said. And then, under her breath, "That having children is a pain in the arse."

II. WALLFLOWER AND CASANOVA

Layla ran.

Her aching feet carried her across the cracked, buckled pavement of their own accord, her lungs sucked in the smoky air and pushed it back out, and the stitch in her side cried out for her to stop, but still she ran.

She snapped her head around quickly, terrified of tripping, but desperate to see if her colleagues were still there. She was alone. Alicia and Sarah were gone. There was no sign of either of them. Layla tried to remember the last time she was sure they'd been behind her, but everything was a swirling, nightmarish blur.

If they were still alive, maybe she'd somehow find them again. If they were dead, there would be time to mourn them later.

For now, she ran.

The sounds of chaos grew fainter, but they still spurred her on. Screams, explosions, sirens, and concussive blasts filled the night air. Her city was in its death throes.

Massive skyscrapers were smashed or completely leveled. The sky was lit by raging fires. Walking among the buildings, each step an earthquake of its own, were impossibly huge robots, their reflective hides gleaming in the destruction as they made their way systematically, block by block, decimating anything and anyone in their path.

A sudden whooshing sound over her head made her come to a skidding, ungainly halt. She felt a surge of adrenaline as squad after squad of hyperjets filled the visible sky above, swarming past her, loaded with laser fire and concussion missiles. Every instinct told her to get moving again, keep putting distance between herself and the robots, but she stood on the splintered double yellow line and watched as salvation flew toward chaos.

And she saw the nearest robot swat the entire attacking force out of the sky with one swing of its massive arm before any of them even fired a shot.

So Layla ran again, sprinting down the same broken street, in one direction only, away from the destruction. She ran block after block, sweating, crying, not knowing where she was going and not really caring, only that she was moving toward relative safety. If there still was such a thing.

As she put more city blocks between herself and the fiery wreckage that used to be her home, the streetlamps suddenly shut off and the streets plunged into darkness. Her left foot caught on something and she tripped at full speed, landing hard as her shoulder hit the unforgiving pavement.

She cried out, and her voice echoed back to her from the pitch blackness between the massive skyscrapers. Then the streetlights flickered back to life, feebly, and she was able to see her surroundings.

There was a darkened, abandoned deli with a cracked front window directly ahead of her, and she crawled gingerly over to the doorway, her shoulder smarting. As she moved, she cast her gaze back toward the way she'd come. The robots, shining white and orange among the flames, were still visible, moving meticulously, street by street, unstoppable death machines.

In the doorway she sat down, her aching legs screaming at the sudden new position, her breath coming in labored gasps, and peered at the glass front door. Her ghostly reflection stared back at her—the same plain, unremarkable face she usually saw, only now it was streaked with grime, blood, and ash. Her black jumpsuit had torn at the shoulder, just above the stitched caduceus in gold.

She got clumsily to her feet, hands on her knees, and waited for her breath to come back. The adrenaline was beginning to wear off, and her shoulder ached like a rotten tooth.

"Five minutes," she croaked.

Five minutes passed and, cradling her bad arm, she stood up and crossed out into the middle of the abandoned pavement. She was just about to take her first running steps when she heard a very faint mewling noise, coming from across the street. She paused.

The sound was coming from a smashed, abandoned daycare center.

Layla crossed the street, and as she reached the front of

the building, she realized there wasn't just one sound, but several. She shoved her good shoulder against the door. It gave a bit, so she shoved harder a few more times and it finally opened enough for her to squeeze in.

She unzipped the field pack resting on her hip and dug out a head lamp. She clicked it to life and looked around.

The ceiling inside the center had collapsed, and trapped among the debris were dozens of children, most of whom looked to still be alive, but badly wounded. Layla froze, unable to process what she was seeing. Her own aches and pains suddenly vanished as the reality of the situation washed over her.

"Oh my God," she whispered.

She ran over to the closest child, an unconscious young boy with a bleeding head wound. She removed her field pack and dug frantically in it, finally pulling out an earpiece communicator. She hooked it on her ear and tapped it.

"Priority one, medical emergency!" she cried. "Any med-vacs, please respond!"

She dug further into the field pack and found a small silver disk, the size of a quarter. Her hands shaking, she attached it as gently as she could to the wound on the boy's head. The disk came to life, injecting topical anesthetic at the wound site and starting to stitch it up. She dug out another device and attached it to his wrist, where it immediately began pumping blood into his veins.

"Any med-vacs, please respond!" Layla shouted again, a tinge of panic in her voice now.

She moved to the next child, a boy with both legs twisted the wrong way.

"Please?" she said, her voice cracking.

She heard a buzz of static in her ear and then a man's deep voice. "*This is med-vac nine responding.*"

Layla put her hand to her mouth and burst into grateful tears.

"*What's your status?*"

"I'm at a daycare center somewhere on 121st street," Layla said, sniffling and dabbing her eyes with her shirt cuff. "I have approximately three dozen wounded children. I'm in triage now."

"*Someone abandoned a bunch of children?*" the voice said, sounding incredulous.

"It looks that way."

"*Jesus. Copy that, I am locked onto your signal and inbound. ETA, four minutes.*"

"Thank you. Er, roger that."

Layla moved on to the next child, a little blonde girl who was barely conscious. As she shifted her light, Layla saw that the girl's left arm was nearly severed at the shoulder. She let out a small shriek at the sight of the copious amounts of blood. The voice crackled in once again.

"*You all right, miss?*"

Layla bit her lower lip hard and tried to regain her composure.

"Yes," she said shakily. "They're just ... they're hurt really bad."

"*It's okay. Just keep doing what you're doing.*"

"I don't ... I don't know ..."

"*Easy. It's all right. Do what you can. I'm on my way,*" said the voice reassuringly.

"Right."

Layla took a deep breath, felt around in her field pack, and started tending to the little girl.

"*So are you a doctor?*" the voice asked suddenly.

"I'm sorry?"

"*I asked if you were a doctor.*"

"Oh," Layla said. "No. A nurse. Barely."

"*How are you barely a nurse?*"

"I just graduated nursing school a month ago."

"*Oh. Well, welcome to the big time.*"

Layla couldn't help but grin a bit. "And you," she said. "You're a pilot?"

"*Among other things, yes.*"

"Do you ... do you have a name, pilot?"

"*My call sign is Casanova.*"

"Why's that?"

A pause, and then: "*That's a longer story for another time.*"

Outside the daycare center, Layla heard the roar of approaching engines, and then the familiar whine as they switched to hover mode. In her mind's eye she could see it: a white medical hyperjet with a large red cross on the belly and the sides, floating gently over the building.

"*I'm at your location,*" Casanova said. "*Start wrapping the packages.*"

Layla moved back to the first child she tended to, and was enormously relieved at how much more stable he looked. Digging in a separate pouch in her field pack, she pulled out a glowing purple bracelet.

"Copy that."

She placed the bracelet on the boy's wrist and watched as

he was suddenly wrapped in a purple cocoon of energy.

"First package is wrapped," she said.

"*Copy that,*" replied Casanova.

The cocoon glowed steadily brighter and the boy suddenly vanished.

"*Package is secure,*" said Casanova.

"Copy. Stand by."

"*You're doing great,*" he said. "*You got a name?*"

"Nothing as colorful as Casanova."

"*What, you never had a nickname?*"

Layla couldn't suppress a wry grin.

"In nursing school they called me Wallflower."

"*Oh yeah?*" he said. She thought she could hear him smile through her earpiece. "*Why's that?*"

"Because of the trouble I had talking to men."

After a momentary pause, they both burst out laughing.

"*Okay, Wallflower it is. How are we doing?*"

"Getting there. What's the latest on the battle?" Layla asked.

"*Battle? Oh, you mean the big metal things annihilating the city while we helplessly watch?*"

"Yeah. That's the one."

"*Pretty good.*"

Layla crawled over to the next child, a small boy trapped under a support beam. Layla shifted the beam off of him with a grunt and saw that he was bleeding from the mouth.

"I want my mother," said the boy, weakly.

"Shhh, you're gonna be all right," Layla said. "I'm gonna get you out of here."

The boy nodded. Layla attached a silver disk to the boy's

abdomen and let it do its work. She moved over to one of the stabilized children and slapped a bracelet on. In a purple glow, the child vanished.

"You still with me, Casanova?" Layla asked.

"Not going anywhere."

"I suppose you think that since we're sharing this intense experience, I'm going to fall hopelessly in love with you."

"That's the plan."

Layla smiled.

"Well, not a chance. You at least have to buy me dinner first."

"Copy that. I know a great little sidewalk bistro on Fourth Street. Well, now it's probably on Fourth, Fifth, and Sixth Streets."

Layla snickered. Just as she reached the next child, a massive concussion in the distance rattled the building. Chunks of the ceiling and clouds of dust rained down. Through her earpiece, Layla heard the strident beeping of an alarm in Casanova's cockpit.

"What was that?" she cried.

"One of the robots has broken off its east-west route and is now headed due north. It's coming straight toward us."

"Oh God," Layla said. "How much time do we have?"

"Less than five minutes."

Layla looked around the room at all the children she hadn't even reached yet. Panic, raw and electric, suddenly overwhelmed her.

"There's too many! There's too many! I'll never get them all out in time!"

"Wallflower, listen to me," Casanova said calmly. *"Do not panic, do you copy? Do not panic."*

"What do I do?" she whimpered.

"Okay, we don't have enough time to stabilize them, so I want you to wrap all the rest of the packages now. Do you understand? I don't care what kind of shape they're in."

"Okay. Okay."

Layla upended her field pack and spilled out all the remaining bracelets. She began slapping them on wrists as fast as she could. Another concussion, louder this time, knocked her off her feet and brought more of the ceiling down.

"Talk to me, Wallflower!"

"Six more!"

Layla slapped bracelets on three more children and they disappeared. The other three children were on the far side of a pile of rubble. She began to crawl over it.

"Two minutes!" Casanova shouted.

Another concussion, the loudest yet, knocked Layla from the top of the rubble pile, right down to the children she was trying to reach. She looked at them and then looked at the bracelets in her hand. Three kids. Three bracelets.

The dawning realization send a cold drop of terror into her belly. Knowing there was nothing to be done about it, in quick succession, she slapped the bracelets on the remaining children. They glowed in their cocoons and, one by one, vanished. She started to weep, but managed to croak out the words to Casanova.

"Last one!"

"Great job!" Casanova yelled. *"Now package yourself up and let's get the hell out of here."*

She was crying so hard she could barely get the words out.

"No. I mean last one," she croaked. "Last bracelet."

There was a palpable silence between them.

"Oh God."

"Go!" she cried. "Get them somewhere safe."

Casanova paused. *"I can land. I can pick you up."*

"There's no time! Go!"

"Wallflower ..."

"Layla. My name's Layla. Now get out of here."

Outside, she heard the medical hyperjet roar away, followed by the sound of what could only be a giant robot's foot smashing down into the pavement a block away from the building.

Layla, her tears cutting tracks through the smeared dirt on her face, walked slowly out of the building, prepared to meet her fate. She threw down her field pack in frustration ...

... and a lone bracelet tumbled out into the rubble.

She stared at it in disbelief, and then scooped it up and ran out into the street. Once outside, she slapped the bracelet onto her wrist and tapped her ear communicator.

"Casanova! Casanova, do you copy?" she cried.

She turned and saw an impossibly massive mechanized foot rise up into the air.

"Casanova?"

Layla was suddenly wrapped in a cocoon of purple energy as the foot came down and smashed the street into oblivion.

III. JOHNNY ON THE SPOT

"Johnny?"

Johnny turned and saw Mr. Eubanks, the president of Eubanks Savings & Loan, approaching from his office in the back. The bank was deathly silent. No one had been to work in days. Mr. Eubanks' footfalls echoed off the marble floors.

"Mr. Eubanks," Johnny nodded.

"Johnny," Mr. Eubanks said, looking around at the deserted lobby, "what are you doing here?"

"I work here," Johnny said. "I don't know if I ever told you this, but it was your great-grandfather who first gave me my job here. I remember it was the winter of '69—or maybe it was '70. Anyway, I had just gotten back from Vietnam, and I heard that old man Eubanks was looking for a bank guard. I came in to talk to him, he took one look at my crew cut, and hired me on the spot. Heh. 'Go out there and guard my money,' he used to say to me. He passed away in '77 or so. Good fella, old man Eubanks was. There was this one time, he had just hired a teller with the most enormous—"

"Yes, yes, I've heard that story," Mr. Eubanks interrupted.

Johnny stared off in the distance and a big smile spread across his face. "Mmmm. They surely don't throw Christmas parties like that anymore."

"No, thankfully not," Mr. Eubanks said curtly. "But back to my original question. What are you doing here?"

"I'm here every day, sir. Like clockwork. You know that. Did you know that I had a hip replacement and never took a single day off? I waited until Christmas fell on a Friday—in '88 or '89 that was—and I took the long weekend to recuperate. I was back here at my post first thing Monday morning. Sore, mind you, and a bit late. Five minutes. But here."

Mr. Eubanks' demeanor softened. "Johnny ... you've heard the news, haven't you?"

"I bring the paper in with me every day," Johnny said, nodding toward the folded newspaper on a small table next to him. "Reminds me of when I had a paper route as a boy. That must have been, oh, back in '59 or so. I was one of the few kids in the neighborhood to own a bicycle, so I could deliver papers the fastest of anyone on the block."

"So then you know there's only a few days left," Mr. Eubanks said softly. "I mean, for everyone."

Johnny straightened his back. "I know."

Mr. Eubanks gestured toward all the empty teller spots. "That's why no one's here. They're all off spending their final days as they see fit."

Johnny smiled. "Yeah, I spoke to Carol last week. She said she was going to go to New Mexico. Always wanted to go to

New Mexico, she said. I told her I've heard it's beautiful this time of year."

"Well ... isn't there anyplace you want to go? Anything you want to do before ... before it's over?" Mr. Eubanks asked.

"Mr. Eubanks," Johnny said, "all I've ever wanted to do is show up for work, on time, every day, and do a good job. I don't have any family, all my friends are long in their graves, and I only ever went on one vacation, to Niagara Falls with my folks when I was a kid. I hated it. So unless I'm fired, I'm going to stand my post, as I've done for the past 39 years, and stand it well."

Mr. Eubanks regarded Johnny for a moment, and then extended his hand. Johnny shook it. Then Eubanks looked at his watch.

"Eleven o'clock. About time for your break, isn't it?" Mr. Eubanks said.

"Yes sir, it is," Johnny said.

Mr. Eubanks walked over to one of the abandoned offices, grabbed two chairs, and dragged them back to where Johnny stood. He arranged them facing each other, sat in one, and gestured for Johnny to sit in the other. After a moment's hesitation, Johnny sat.

"So tell me more about my great-grandfather," Mr. Eubanks said.

"Oh, old man Eubanks was a hot ticket," Johnny said. "I remember once a gentleman came into the bank and claimed one of the tellers had short-changed him. Well, old man Eubanks counted out the drawer to prove the man was lying, but the man demanded restitution. Things got heated, all right. I was all ready to step in, but the next thing I know old man   Eubanks   balls   up   his   fist,   and   *wham*!"

IV. RUNNING ON EMPTY

The early morning sun peeked over the treetops and raised the frosty temperature a few welcome degrees. Maria closed her eyes and turned her face gratefully upward to feel the heat on her pink nose and apple cheeks.

She let her eyelids drift lazily up, turned her face away from the welcome sun, and looked around at the thousands of people all gathered near the festive START banner. Most of them were stretching. Or jogging. Or otherwise rubbing their physical fitness in Maria's face. She hated every expensive sneaker and tight butt she saw.

Not that she had cheap sneakers or a butt that wouldn't one day be tight. But Maria's journey had been a long one, from formless blob on the couch eating her way into an early grave to a regular, if initially embarrassed, attendee at the local gym where the men would look at her like a stray dog off the street, to a by-God race runner. None of it been easy, and she wouldn't wish those first few exercise sessions on her worst enemy. But she was down from a mortifying 400 pounds to 221 (which she rounded right down to 220, thank you very much) and was just about 20 minutes away from running her very first marathon.

It wasn't one of those big, national marathons. There wouldn't be television cameras or a writeup in the paper tomorrow. It was just a local event. But it was still a marathon, dammit, and she was running it.

A *marathon*. She turned the word over and over in her head and couldn't find a way to assign it to herself. Just over 26 miles. Jesus.

A voice on a bullhorn rang out on the still morning air, reminding everyone that the race would be starting shortly. A quick thought shot across Maria's mind: *I can't do this.* She quashed the thought before it could take hold. She was going to do this. She was going to do this.

The hands on her watch spun of their own accord, at their own speed, and before she knew it, she was lined up near the middle of the pack, taking deep breaths and exhaling them as steam in the cold air. The moment drew nearer. Three minutes.

Two.

One.

The starter pistol cracked and suddenly the air was filled with the sound of rubber soles slapping the asphalt, including Maria's. As she passed the start line, her heart leapt.

I'm running a marathon!

She found the first mile horribly claustrophobic. The pack was tight. She kept her elbows in at her sides and watched the feet of the runner in front of her, worried that she'd catch his heel with her toe and cause a massive pileup of bodies.

Slowly but surely, the pack loosened as the runners found their own paces and gaits, and Maria was able to relax enough to find her own groove. The course thus far was fast and flat, and for that she was immeasurably thankful, though she was certain it wouldn't last forever.

As she passed into the second mile, she noticed that her breath was coming in big whoops and gasps. This was something new. She'd trained hard on tougher courses and learned to control her breathing. She chalked it up to nerves and focused on keeping her pace.

The road unrolled before her, the cracked and faded yellow line her constant companion. A few groups of spectators applauded the runners as they made their way past, but it seemed that for most, it was either too early or too cold. Or both.

Along the sides of the road were dense clusters of trees, and as the race moved on, the first few birds of dawn began to twitter in the branches.

The road curved sharply around a curve to the left, and as Maria rounded it, she could see for a good mile or two ahead.

There were hills. Lots of them.

She had trained on hills, and she had her technique down for hills, but she still didn't like them. As the first rise approached, slowly, insidiously, she felt the first few beads of sweat popping up on her brow and rolling down her back, to her butt that was not yet tight.

The hills continued, and so did Maria.

The race went on.

To keep herself occupied, Maria thought about the first time she ran. It was right after a physical, and her doctor had given her a dire list of things that almost certainly would happen to her and then another equally dire list of things that *could* happen if she didn't do something about her sedentary lifestyle. She told her doctor that she was forty-three years old and it was too late for her to do anything. Her doctor was a firm believer that it was never too late.

So that night, just after sunset so that it would be harder for the neighbors to see her massive bulk jiggling along the sidewalk, Maria ran. She barely made it 20 feet. Everything hurt. Her boobs bounced and flapped on the top of her belly. Her thighs felt like two sticks she'd rubbed together to make fire. One of her sneakers had come untied and it was going to stay untied until she figured out the physics of contorting her body to allow her to tie it again.

She looked over her shoulder at her little house, the lights warm and inviting, her long-suffering couch just waiting for her return. Then she looked back at the street ahead, dark, unforgiving, and mocking her. And with her boobs flapping, her thighs rubbing, and one shoe untied, she kept running.

The race passed in a monotone, foot after foot, hill after hill, mile after endless mile. Just after she passed the mile nine marker, Maria took stock of herself. Her feet were reasonably pain-free, though she could feel something on the outside of her right big toe that might prove to be a problem before too long. She couldn't really feel her legs; they seemed to be moving on their own, which was just fine by her. Her back and her shoulders were sore, but the pain was manageable.

The real problem was her lungs.

She had given up the illusion that her trouble breathing was marathon jitters. She was panting like an old dog on a hot day. No matter how deeply she pulled in breath, she couldn't seem to get enough air, and she was starting to feel the first jolts of panic. The last thing she wanted to do was slow down or stop—not just because it would be so hard to get going again, but because she'd made a promise to herself that she would run the whole thing. So she ran on, taking in big gulps of air and heaving them back out.

The next few miles were agony. Her breathing became more and more labored, to the point where other runners were starting to look at her with expressions of genuine concern. She waved them off with a strained smile and kept going.

By mile fourteen, she was edging dangerously close to hyperventilation and her heart was hammering in her chest. And still she pushed.

"Five minutes," she huffed. "Just run ... for five more minutes."

As she crested a small hill, Maria's vision suddenly doubled and dizziness overtook her. She came to a halting, ungainly stop as black spots crossed her field of vision and the world began to fade to black. She was pitching sideways when she suddenly felt a strong hand in the crook of her elbow.

"Whoa!" she heard a man's voice say. "Easy now."

She opened her eyes and saw a fellow runner standing next to her. He was extremely tall and gangly, with a pronounced nose and Adam's apple, and a ridiculous red, white, and blue headband in his longish, dark hair. Despite that, he was quite good-looking, with such a smooth face that she couldn't possibly guess his age. With one hand he was holding her up, keeping her from collapse, steadying her on her feet.

"Are you okay?" he said kindly.

She shook her head as she wheezed and gasped. "Can't … do this …" she managed.

"Nonsense," the man said. He didn't say it in an accusatory way, merely mild disbelief that a simple thing like finishing a marathon somehow wasn't possible. "Come on, I'll run with you."

She shook her head and wheezed, "No. I'm … finished. Go … you're wasting … time."

"Oh, don't worry about me," the man said with a grin. "I've got all the time in the world."

He kept hold of her elbow and guided her over to the side of the road, where she took hold of the crowd barrier and lowered her head, waiting for the dizziness to completely pass. It did, but very slowly, and her breath was still ragged.

A wave of fury hit her, white hot and electric, and she kicked the metal barrier in a fit of frustration. It didn't seem to help much, so she grabbed the barrier, lifted the end of it as high as she could, and smashed it over and over again on the pavement. It made a satisfyingly loud clang, which made her feel marginally better, but drew curious and alarmed stares from the runners who were passing by.

"*What're you looking at!*" she screamed at the very top of her lungs, and the other marathoners gave her a wide berth. She felt angry tears tracking down her cheeks. She shoved the barrier aside and sat down hard on the stone curb behind it, head down and arms folded, and let more tears come.

"Well, glad you got that out of your system," the man who had helped her said conversationally. She looked up to see his gangly form standing over her. "Are you ready to get going again? Finish this thing?"

"I'm not *finishing this thing*!" she lashed out savagely. "Go away! Leave me alone!"

The man didn't move. Runners were passing him by, but he stood there, watching her.

"So what's your plan, then?" he asked quietly.

"I told you to leave me alone!" she spat.

"Oh, I heard you," he said. He looked to his left. "I think they probably heard you at the finish line. I still want to know what your plan is."

Maria didn't respond. Her heart was pounding and she could hear her blood coursing in her ears. Her breath was still frustratingly short. She stared miserably at the patch of asphalt between her feet.

"Okay, well," he said, taking a seat on the curb next to her, "I guess I'll just make myself comfortable then."

"Why won't you leave me alone?" she said, her voice quavering.

"Because I'm not entirely sure you know what you're going to do if you don't run this race," he said.

She took in a deep, shuddering breath and blew it back out. She turned to him. He had such a kind face, she couldn't bring herself to shout at him any more.

"Fine," she said. "I'm going to sit here on this curb until the marathon is over. And then when they open the road again, I'll hitch a ride home. There. Are you satisfied? Will you go away now, please?"

He stared at her for a few moments, sizing her up. Then he shook his head.

"Nope, sorry," he said. "That's not going to work for me. In fact, of all the plans I've ever heard in my life, that has to be right up there with the worst of them."

"What do you care?" she asked. She had never felt so drained in her entire life, and the last thing she wanted was to be stuck talking to someone. "What do you care what happens to me?"

"What a strange question," the man said. "Tell me something. If the shoe were on the other foot, and I was sitting here, refusing to finish this marathon, talking about hitching a ride home with a potential serial killer an indeterminate amount of time from now, would you honestly not care about any of that?"

Maria didn't have to think it over. Of course she would care. He seemed to read that on her face.

"All right then," he said.

They sat in silence as the race passed by, and the steady stream of runners began to trickle off.

"You know what's fun?" the man said at last.

Maria didn't respond.

"Walking," the man said. "Nothing like a good walk, am I right?"

Maria merely shrugged.

"Yes, I find that when I'm not in the mood for a run, a walk is just as good," he said. "Sometimes better."

She cottoned on to what he was suggesting and rolled her

eyes at him.

"I'm not walking a marathon," she said flatly.

"Well, no, you wouldn't be," he replied. "You'd be walking less than half a marathon. You already ran most of it."

Maria looked at the man for a long while, and he didn't look away.

"I told you," she said, but softer now. "I can't do this. I can't breathe."

"Oh, how much breath does it take to walk?" he said, capitalizing on his advantage and getting to his feet.

"It can still take a lot," she said.

"Not if we walk slowly," he said with a smile, and offered her his hand. She shook her head, but then put her palm against his and allowed him to pull her to her feet.

"All right," she said, but immediately put her finger up. "But slowly. I'm not kidding."

"Wonderful!" he said, and the amount of joy he showed at her decision took her aback. They started walking slowly, side by side, as the last of the runners began to pass them both by. "I'm Gabe. What's your name?"

"Maria," she said sulkily. Watching the other runners keep going was quickly getting under her skin.

"Maria," he said, and then suddenly sang in a surprisingly powerful tenor voice, "*I just met a girl named Mariiiaaaa ...*"

She was so surprised that she momentarily forgot all the people passing them by, and even forgot that they were still walking, though her breath was already failing her again, even at such a slow pace.

"Where you from?"

"Bal ... Baltimore," she said, swallowing air.

"Oh, lovely city," Gabe said with a smile. "Y'know, if you like dumps."

Maria smiled.

"Hey," she panted. "That's … my hometown … you're talking about."

"Well," Gabe said. "I'll try not to hold that against you."

The scenery moved slowly along with them, and some spectators cheered them as they went, even though they were walking. Maria felt her spirits lift and waved at them. Gabe followed suit.

"So what do you do in Baltimore?" he asked.

"I'm a housekeeper. At a hotel," she replied.

"Ah," Gabe said. "So you're one of those people who insists on waking me up at six in the morning when I clearly have the Do Not Disturb door hanger hanging." He imitated knocking on a door, and in a high-pitched voice shrieked, *"Ousekeeping! Ousekeeping!"*

Maria giggled. "Sounds just like me."

They passed through a bright patch of sunlight peeking through the trees and then back into rippling shadows.

"Hey," Gabe said after a while. "Look at that."

In the distance, Maria could see the mile fifteen marker sitting on the shoulder.

"I bet," Gabe said, "if we continued walking to the sign, and then after the sign jogged very, very slowly, we'd be all right."

Icy panic coursed through Maria's veins. She stopped and Gabe stopped with her.

"I can't," she said, and there was a pleading, helpless tone in her voice that made her cringe. "Gabe, I can't."

"Okay, okay," Gabe said, taking her hands in his. He smiled. "We'll walk. Okay? We'll walk."

She nodded, and they continued walking.

"This actually works out well," he continued. "I told all my friends that I'd finish this thing in just under three weeks. It'll be close, but I think I'll be able to do it."

Maria smiled again.

"Okay, fine," she said at last. "But a very slow, very light jog."

"The slowest and lightest jog the world has ever seen," Gabe replied.

They passed the mile fifteen marker and Maria broke into a light trot, and Gabe matched her gait. Maria was surprised at how much easier it seemed.

"There we are," said Gabe. "Movin' right along."

Maria nodded, concentrating on her breathing. Even that seemed easier. She thought of all the articles she'd read about runners getting their second wind. Was that all it was?

"So," Gabe said. "Where are you from?"

Maria looked at him quizzically.

"You already asked me that," she said.

Gabe smiled kindly at her. "Humor me."

Maria went to answer, but just as her lips formed the word, she found she suddenly couldn't remember where she was from. Her mind worked furiously, but the name wouldn't come.

"It's all right," Gabe said. "Don't stress about it. What do you do for a living?"

Maria looked at Gabe like he'd lost his sanity. "You already asked me that too!"

"And what did you tell me?"

Again, Maria tried to answer, and again, she drew a complete blank.

"Oh God," she said, reaching out for Gabe's arm for support. "What's happening to me?"

Gabe continued to smile. "You're letting it all go," he said. "There's nothing to be afraid of. This is how it's supposed to happen."

"How *what's* supposed to happen?" Maria demanded.

"I'll see you at the finish line," Gabe replied cryptically, and he put on a sudden burst of speed. He was sprinting ahead so fast that he was practically around the next turn before Maria realized what had happened.

"Wait!" she cried, and before she realized what she was doing, she was sprinting as well. But she felt no pain at all, no fear, no sensation like her lungs were going to explode. The trees and the spectators and the road were all flying by, and she felt nothing but pure elation.

She saw Gabe ahead of her, looking over his shoulder, smiling, beckoning her to run and catch up with him. She was so focused on him and the pure joy she felt that she barely registered coming into the marathon's home stretch.

The FINISH banner stretched across the road and hundreds of people were gathered on either side of the crowd barriers as she ran down the last yards. Some of the faces she passed looked familiar, but her feet were moving so fast that she had no time to wonder if she knew them or not. The end of the race was just past the line ahead, and she flew over it with her arms held up in joyous celebration.

The moment she crossed the finish line, everything froze. The road, the people, the sky, the world—all of it just stopped in a shocking, reverberating silence, like a movie stuck on a single frame. Maria was not afraid, merely curious about what had happened.

How long she stood there, staring at frozen faces, motionless clouds, hands caught in mid-clap, she couldn't say. It could have been minutes or months. She was started out of her reverie by the touch of a hand on her shoulder.

She turned and saw a man, tall and well-built, dressed in a very fashionable black suit, and he had a very youthful face. He reached his hands toward her, and she took them.

"Maria," he said. "At last. Welcome."

A million questions raced through her mind, but she heard herself blurt out, "Who are you?"

"I'm Peter," he said. "It's so nice to finally meet you."

"What's happening?" she asked, looking around her.

"Ah, that's a bit of a tricky question," Peter replied. "The easiest and most straightforward answer I can give you is that you're in the transition. To the afterlife."

"You mean," Maria said heavily, "I'm dead? I'm on my way to heaven?"

"Well, yes, you are dead," Peter replied. "And there's eternal life awaiting you. Whether you choose to call it heaven is entirely up to you."

"But … I just finished running a marathon," Maria said. "How can I be dead?"

"Oh, well, you actually died during the marathon," Peter said. "Do you remember a point where you were very dizzy and blacked out for a moment?"

"Yes."

"Brain aneurysm," Peter said. "It was very quick."

Maria was shaking her head. "No, that's not right," she protested. "I got dizzy, and then Gabe showed up to help me."

Peter took a deep breath. "Maria, this is a lot to take in. Are you sure you wouldn't like to get your legs under you a bit before trying to understand it all?"

"No, please," she said. "Tell me."

"Very well," Peter said. "As I said, you suffered a fatal brain aneurysm just after mile fourteen of the marathon. You should have come directly here, to the transition, but you wouldn't allow yourself to."

"Why not?" she asked.

"Because you hadn't completed the race," Peter explained. "You felt you still had unfinished business. But you didn't believe that you *could* finish the race, so you were stuck in a sort of limbo. For quite some time."

"What does that mean?" she said. "How long?"

"Maria, what year is it?"

"It's 1975," she said.

"Mmmm," Peter nodded. "Let's just say that an awful lot of time has passed and leave it at that."

"But if that's true … if I was stuck for so long, how did I finally get here?"

"Oh, well, that was Gabe," Peter said, smiling. "He is, for lack of a better term, your guardian angel."

"He is?" Maria said wonderingly.

"Oh yes. He spent years, decades trying to find you and help you finish what you started. He finally succeeded. And here you are."

Maria suddenly felt a deep sense of shame. "I was so awful to him."

"Eh, I've had worse," Gabe said, materializing out of nowhere.

"Gabe!" Maria cried, throwing her arms around his neck. She hugged him as tightly as she could and he hugged her right back.

They drew apart. "Nice to finally see you here."

"It's nice to be here," Maria laughed. "So you guided me to the finish line?"

"Well, you just got a little stuck along the way," Gabe said. "It's more like I nudged you and got you moving again. That's all."

"During the race," she said, "you started asking me the same questions you asked me before. And I couldn't answer them."

"That's part of the process," Gabe replied. "Before you can get here, you have to let go of everything that binds you to your previous life."

"Is that why I was able to run so fast?" Maria asked. "Because I was letting go of my fear of failure? Of my doubt?"

"Exactly," Gabe said.

Maria turned to Peter. "So now what?"

"Oh, well, now you move on," he said matter-of-factly.

"Move on to where?"

"That's ... also a little tough to explain. Probably best that you see for yourself."

He gestured down the road, past the finish area, and as

Maria watched in awe, two doors suddenly opened out of nowhere at a point off in the distance. Burning light poured out from beyond them.

"There are an awful lot of people waiting to say hello," Peter said, smiling. "Best to not keep them waiting."

Gabe gave Maria a small nudge and she turned to him.

"C'mon," he said with a grin. "I'll race ya."

V. THE HAUNTING OF FLATTOP HARRIS

They didn't know it then, but four young men were about to have their lives changed forever.

They were sitting respectfully in their seats in the old auditorium, seniors at the end of the school year, finally about to graduate high school and make their way out into the real world. But for the moment, they were watching Lieutenant Shipley, an army officer impressive in full dress uniform, as he mesmerized them with his polished and well-rehearsed speech.

"People ask me all the time," Lieutenant Shipley said, his voice so deep and powerful that he barely needed the microphone, "what is patriotism? Well, I'll make it easy for you. Do you love your country?"

He pointed the microphone at the crowd and theatrically cupped his ear.

"Yes!" the kids yelled in reply.

"Do you support your country?"

"Yes!"

"Are you loyal to your country?"

"Yes!"

"And would you defend your country with your life?"

"Yes!"

"Well that's patriotism, right there," Shipley said, flashing a winning smile. "And if you want to be a true patriot, I urge you to consider a career in the military."

Pre-recorded patriotic music warbled out of the dusty old speakers on either side of the stage.

"As we speak, brave men and women are on their way over to Korea to fight the forces of communism. And if you want to be among them, standing shoulder to shoulder with America's finest, the military can make it happen. I thank you all for your time and attention, and God bless America."

Shipley snapped into a tight, formal salute as the music reached its crescendo, all trumpets and crashing cymbals. The students, as one, leapt to their feet and applauded wildly. The four boys looked at one another, their eyes alight.

In the schoolyard a short while later, Flattop Harris walked across the hot black asphalt with Ricky, Tommy, and Jake. The other three were talking animatedly, but Flattop walked with his head down, hands in his pockets, the sun lighting up his flaming red buzz cut as it deposited a few more freckles across his cheeks and nose.

"So whaddya think?" said Ricky, turning to the other three.

"I'm signin' up, no question. You?" said Tommy.

"Without a doubt! I'm gonna be a patriot! Take that, ya lousy Koreens!" Ricky replied, throwing an uppercut at the air in front of him. "Jake?"

"I'll have to talk it over with my pop, but he served in the Big One. I'm sure he'll be thrilled with the idea. What about you, Flattop?" said Jake.

Flattop said nothing.

"Well c'mon, Flattop. Whaddya say? The Four Musketeers! It'll be just like it was at summer camp!"

"Hey, you think they'll let us serve together? Like in the same unit?" said Ricky.

"Hey yeah! They just might! If we all sign up together, that is," said Tommy.

"That sound good to you, Flattop?" said Jake.

Flattop continued to walk, silent. Jake grabbed him by the arm and stopped him.

"What's eatin' you, anyway?" demanded Jake.

Flattop looked around at the others. His three best friends for as long as he could remember. It was tough for him to say it.

"Look, it ain't like I'm a coward or nothin'. And it ain't like I don't believe in patriotism. It's just that ..." said Flattop, trailing off.

"Well spit it out. It's just that what?" said Jake.

"Well it ain't like it is in the movies, y'know? It ain't like it is in the comic books neither. If you get killed in a war, you get killed. You're dead. That's it. You ain't comin' back. No parades. No award ceremonies. No nothin'. You're just dead is all."

They all stared at him in silence, mulling over his words.

"I got things I wanna do in my life, y'know? And I can't do 'em if I go and get myself killed."

"Well then you just make sure you don't get killed. Right?" asked Tommy.

Flattop's cheeks flushed suddenly red.

"Well it ain't always up to you, is it?" he shouted.

No one had an answer to that. Uncomfortable silence fell among them, until at last, Jake spoke up.

"Well, look, it ain't like we gotta sign up today or nothin'. Just think it over, willya Flattop?" he said.

Flattop nodded.

"Hey, pickup game over in Old Man Hennigan's field?" Tommy asked brightly. Flattop nodded again, but this time with a smile, and the four of them headed out of the schoolyard.

On a darkened road at the north end of town, a solitary toll booth sat on a stretch of two-lane blacktop with very little traffic to even warrant its existence.

With only the company of bugs bouncing off the floodlights, Flattop perched on an uncomfortable wooden stool in the steel-and-glass coffin, engrossed in a college textbook. He hardly noticed the rumbling engine of an approaching pickup truck until it wheezed into silence just outside his window.

Flattop bookmarked his page and slid the window open. Sitting in the driver's seat was a farmer so old and weathered that his skin had the look of a dusty field desperate for rain. His lips were collapsed in over his toothless gums, and a battered old baseball cap shaded his deep-set eyes. Riding shotgun was a bored-looking old basset hound with a pot belly and a patch of white around his left eye that looked like a monocle.

Flattop smiled at the pair. "Evenin', Mister Hennigan," he said brightly. "Evenin', Clutch."

The dog turned for a moment at the sound of his name, then turned back and stared through the dirt-coated windshield.

"Evenin', Flattop," Mister Hennigan said. "How's tricks?"

"Well, things are a little slow," Flattop said, looking both ways down the deserted road.

The old man wheezed laughter. "I reckon so," he said. "I reckon so."

Mister Hennigan looked around, as though expecting to see other people gathered near the toll booth.

"Where're your friends?" he asked.

"My friends?"

"Yeah, them boys you used to pal around with," Hennigan said.

"Oh, those fellas," Flattop said, cottoning on. "Joined up. Army."

"Not you, though, eh?" Hennigan asked. It wasn't accusatory, simply a statement.

"Not me," Flattop said. "I'm enrolled up the college." He grabbed his textbook and gave it a little wave.

Hennigan nodded. "Good for you," he said. "Get your diploma and get the hell outta this shitsplat ol' town."

Flattop grinned. "That's the plan."

Hennigan nodded, and then leaned to his side to dig in the pocket of his ancient overalls. He produced a dime, which he tossed in the basket just below Flattop's window. The barrier across the road slowly lifted.

"You stay outta trouble, now," Hennigan said as he ratcheted the pickup back to life.

"I'll do my best," Flattop said, and waved the old man through as he went on his way.

The next few hours passed quietly. A young man in a gleaming fire-engine-red New Yorker came through, so nervous about the smiling blonde in the passenger seat that he tossed three dimes at the basket before finally landing one in it. Old Lady Higgins came rolling out of the darkness on her rusty old bicycle and asked Flattop, as she did every time she passed, if she needed to pay the toll.

"It's fine, Mrs. Higgins," Flattop said patiently. "You can use the shoulder and go around."

"Oh, thank you dear," Mrs. Higgins said as she trundled off into the dirt and sand on the far side of the road. "What a nice young man."

Midnight approached. Flattop's head rested on his hand and his eyelids drooped as he tried to keep reading his textbook. He heard an approaching car and saw headlights cutting through the darkness, so he once again bookmarked his place, yawned, and stretched.

The bright white star on the vehicle's hood caught his attention, and it was a few moments before his sleepy brain made the connection that it was an army jeep. In it, looking resplendent in their army dress uniforms, were Tommy, Ricky, and Jake, their scalps gleaming pink under their crew cuts.

"Heya, Flattop," said Jake.

Flattop slid the booth window open.

"Well, well, well. Hey there, fellas. Lookin' good."

"Thanks. See you got yourself a little job," said Jake. The statement was laced with thinly veiled contempt.

"Yeah, well. Helps pay for school, y'know." Flattop let the statement breathe for a moment, then pressed on. "So. Ain't seen much of you since graduation."

"Yeah, well, we been over to Fort Benning, ain't we?" said Tommy.

"Yeah, I 'spose you have. So, you're done with basic then?"

"Yep," said Ricky.

"Got your orders yet?"

"Yes indeed. We ship out to Korea on Thursday. We're gonna be servin' under Lieutenant Shipley," said Ricky.

"The speaker from school?"

"The very one."

"Huh. Ain't that somethin'."

"Yes sir. The Three Musketeers," said Ricky, putting the emphasis on "Three." He patted the other two on the shoulders. An uncomfortable silence spun out, pregnant with the sudden and unexpected distance between them.

Jake dug into his pocket and pulled out a dime. He flipped it deftly into the coin basket and the barrier ahead of them rose.

"Well. I guess we better get goin'. Gotta go defend your freedom for you. Good to see you, Flattop," said Jake.

"You too. Give 'em hell, boys."

The jeep rolled off and Flattop watched it go.

A year came and went, as years do.

Flattop was still working the toll booth, a new set of college books stacked up at his elbow. It was late. He dozed fitfully on his stool, leaning against the glass. A misty ground fog crept up over the surface of the road.

The same army jeep as before rolled silently up to the toll booth and stopped. As before, in it were Tommy, Ricky, and Jake. They all looked pale and shaken. Under the bright floodlights, they appeared almost to glow.

"Five minutes," Flattop grunted from his slumber. Then he snorted himself awake and looked around. He spotted the jeep and rubbed his eyes. He slid open the window and leaned out.

"Well I'll be damned! If it ain't the proud members of the fightin' 38th! You fellas home on leave?"

None of them spoke. They stared straight ahead into the darkened mist.

"Fellas? Hey. You all right?"

They remained silent for a few moments, and then Jake spoke. His voice was flat, devoid of inflection, and he addressed no one in particular.

"He was right, y'know," said Jake.

"Who was?" asked Ricky.

"Ol' Flattop. He was right. 'Bout war. It ain't like it is in the movies."

"No. It ain't," said Tommy.

Flattop had no idea what to make of what he was hearing.

"Fellas! Jake! Tommy! It's me, Flattop! I'm right here!"

There was no acknowledgement. The three young men stared into nothingness.

46

"What was it he said? 'If you get killed in a war, you get killed. You're dead. That's it. You ain't comin' back.'" said Tommy.

"No parades. No award ceremonies. No nothin'," continued Ricky.

Flattop waved his arms around.

"Hey! Hey!"

There was still no acknowledgement.

"I feel bad," said Jake.

"'Bout what?" asked Tommy.

"How we treated him last time we saw him. Flattop, I mean," said Jake.

"Yeah. Me too," said Tommy.

Shell shock. It's gotta be, Flattop thought to himself.

Ricky suddenly stirred and looked around. It didn't appear that he actually saw anything.

"Hey. What are we doin' here?" asked Ricky.

"I dunno. I guess we ain't done yet," said Jake.

"Ain't done? What else is there to do?" asked Ricky.

Jake looked up. He raised his voice to a shout.

"Flattop! I don't know if you can hear me, but I'm sorry! We all are! We shoulda been better friends to you! We shoulda listened to you!"

His voice dropped back to normal.

"I only wish it wasn't too late."

Flattop suddenly felt all the wind knocked out of him. He sat down hard on his stool and steadied himself on the windowsill.

"Oh God," said Flattop. "Oh no."

He managed to get to his feet and walked unsteadily out of

the booth. He came around to the driver's side of the jeep. There was still no acknowledgement of him at all.

"You were all …" He paused and swallowed hard. "You were all killed in action. Weren't you? That's it, ain't it?"

No response.

"Aw, hell."

Flattop wiped his nose on the back of his hand.

"Patriotism. That's what patriotism'll get you."

Still no response of any kind. Flattop dabbed at his eyes and took a few deep breaths. Then something dawned on him.

"Wellnow, hang on a minute. If you was all killed overseas, what are you doin' here?"

Then it came to him.

"You need me to forgive you."

He stared at his old friends with a sad little smile.

"Aw, Jake. Tommy. Ricky. There was never nothin' to apologize for. There was never any hard feelings. But if you need to hear it, then I'll say it. I forgive you."

All three men finally looked over in Flattop's direction. It didn't appear as though they could see him, but all three were smiling.

Jake dug in his pocket and produced a ghostly coin. He tossed it toward the basket and it passed right through Flattop. Instead of rising, the barrier ahead faded and then disappeared.

"Come on, boys. We still got a long way to go," said Jake.

The jeep rolled silently forward, and as the ground mist wrapped around it, it vanished from sight.

"So long, fellas."

VI. LEMON DROP

Eric sat in the far corner of the restaurant, obsessively looking at his watch. He was early—he was always early—but he hadn't known how torturous the wait was going to be. If he had, he might have gone against his nature and arrived late. Or later, anyway.

He reached into his jacket pocket to check his phone. Right there on his home screen was her picture—Meredith, the girl he'd be meeting shortly. She was pretty. Not pretty in a supermodel way or in a CW Network way, but pretty in a natural way. Certainly the prettiest he'd found on the site.

It was a new dating site, and since he'd found very little on the others, he'd given this one a shot. It was called Only One. The gag was that you could only see one picture, one quote, one favorite movie, and so forth. And the site went to great pains to make sure you didn't contact the other person before meeting them in person for the first time. So all he knew of her was the picture, her name, her astrological sign, and that she liked *The Notebook*. Everything else he'd learn tonight.

The time was ticking toward 7 o'clock. "Five minutes," Eric muttered to himself.

Five minutes later he looked up and saw the hostess leading his date to the table. He felt a twinge of disappointment. She looked exactly like she did in her photo, but no more. She hadn't done anything with her hair, she wasn't wearing any special makeup, and her outfit was fairly casual for the type of restaurant he'd chosen. Still, he couldn't complain—she hadn't misrepresented herself, and some of his other dates had. She was, in every way, the girl in the picture.

"Sorry I'm late," she said as she sat down across from him. "I hate the traffic in this town. I hate this town, come to think of it."

"Oh, no worries," Eric said brightly. "You're here now, that's all that matters."

"I guess," she shrugged. "What kind of food do they serve here?"

"Mostly Middle Eastern dishes," Eric said. "They have a great—"

"I don't like Middle Eastern food," she interrupted.

"Oh. Uh …" he said lamely. "We could always go someplace else."

"No, it's fine," she said.

"Oh. Okay."

Meredith picked up the menu and started reading. Eric watched her for a few moments, and then said, "So. It's nice to meet you in person."

She continued reading the menu.

"Um ... what do you do for a living?" he offered.

"I spend my days hating my job," she replied.

"Oh? Why's that?"

She closed the menu and sighed. "Because they work us like dogs and pay us like crap. I've been looking for another job, but everything else pays like crap too."

"Oh. I see," Eric said. He motioned to the waitress and she came over to take their drink order.

"Hennessey on the rocks," Eric said, with a hint of desperation. "Make it a double."

"And for you?" she said to Meredith.

"Water," Meredith said flatly.

"Okay, I'll be right over with those," the waitress said and headed away.

"So," Eric said. "Do you ... have any family around here?"

"None that I care to see," Meredith said.

"Huh. I, uh, actually have quite a large family that—"

"Yeah, so do I," she jumped in, "but I just can't stand any of them."

"Ah," Eric said.

They fell into silence. Meredith picked up the menu again and perused.

"Is there anything you'd like to know about me?" Eric asked hopefully.

"Sure," she replied.

More silence.

"Anything in particular?"

She shrugged. "Whatever you want."

"Okay, well, I work at Payatt National Bank."

"Oh, I would *hate* that," she said immediately. "I would

hate working in a bank."

He stared at her blankly. "You don't even know what I do there."

"It doesn't matter," she said dismissively. "I would just hate working in a bank. I don't know how you can do it."

Eric gritted his teeth. "Do you have any hobbies? Anything you like to do for fun?"

"Well," she sighed, "I used to go rollerblading. And then last summer I fell and tore my ACL, so I can't do that anymore. Which sucks."

"That's a shame," Eric replied, but his heart wasn't in it. He actually sort of enjoyed the idea of Meredith in pain. And they hadn't even ordered yet.

"Have you seen *The Boyfriend?*" Eric said. "I thought it was one of the funniest movies I've seen in a long time."

"Yeah, I saw it," Meredith said. "I didn't like it."

"Why not?"

"It was stupid."

"All right," he said through a strained smile. "What movies have you seen lately that weren't stupid?"

"Well, I saw *West of Saturn*. That was stupid. I saw that Rob Schneider movie, that was really stupid."

"I met Rob Schneider once," Eric offered up. "At a coffee shop in Hollywood. He used to live in LA and—"

"No he didn't," Meredith said suddenly.

"Um … yes, I'm pretty sure he did."

"No, you're wrong. He's a native New Yorker, he's lived here all his life."

"No, I'm not wrong. When I met him, he told me he was living in LA."

"Whatever," she said. "That's wrong. I know that's wrong."

They lapsed into silence again. Eric's folded hands were white as he squeezed them together.

"You know what?" he said suddenly. "Let's get out of here."

Meredith looked up at him, puzzled. "We haven't ordered yet."

"I know, but you don't like Middle Eastern food anyway, so let's go someplace else." He stood and threw some money on the table for the drinks that they'd never even enjoyed.

They stepped out of the restaurant and onto the sidewalk beyond.

"So where do you want to go?" Meredith asked.

"Back to my place," Eric replied.

"That's a little forward, isn't it?" she said.

He smiled. "Well, I suppose it would be if I were inviting you along. I want to go back to my place, I want you to go back to your place, and I never want to see you again as long as I live. You are, without question, the most depressing, tedious, awful company I've ever known. Good night, and good bye."

Eric turned and walked away from her.

Meredith turned and walked in the opposite direction. "What a jerk," she muttered.

VII. SO TEN MINUTES AGO

It was a lazy Sunday morning, and bright sunlight shone through the kitchen window as Fergal absentmindedly picked at his egg white omelet and organic fruit, his free hand and his focus on his iPad next to his plate.

As he waited for a page to load, he glanced up and across the table at his roommate, Anakin. People said they looked an awful lot alike, but Fergal didn't see it.

Sure, they were both in their early twenties. And they both wore skinny jeans and woven caps, and they both sported glasses with thick black frames. And yes, they both had decent-sized gauges in their earlobes, and they both had tightly trimmed beards. But as Fergal was quick to point out to anyone who would listen, Anakin's beard was *red* and his own was *black*. So get over it already. They were two completely original young men.

He glanced back down at his iPad, which had finally loaded, and he let out an audible gasp.

"Oh my God, did you read this?" said Fergal. Anakin looked up from his chai tea in sudden alarm. "They're shutting down the Coffee Hauzz downtown!"

"Ugh, about time too," replied Anakin, relaxing. "That place was getting so inwardly focused."

Fergal put his hands out pleadingly. "But now where are we supposed to hang out with Declan and St. Paul and Scorpius and Caoimhseach?"

Anakin's brow furrowed. He clearly hadn't considered the dire consequences.

"Oh, wait," Fergal said, scrolling a little further on the screen. "No, okay, we're fine. They're opening a Coffee Hauzzzzzzz at the same location."

Anakin grunted. "Well, that's one disaster averted."

Fergal tapped the screen. "It also says that the Hat Hut is no longer offering college ID discounts. Well that figures."

"Typical," said Anakin.

"You know, everything cool is so fleeting and pyrrhic," said Fergal.

"I know, right?" Anakin replied. "Why not just put a Spencer Gifts on every corner and be done with it?"

They both returned back to their iPads and continued reading and scrolling.

After breakfast, Fergal stood and stretched as Anakin perused a website that specialized in hemp bracelets and offered free shipping in envelopes that contained seeds and were biodegradable. Fergal was just about to suggest that they go someplace other than the mall when he noticed movement in the adjoining dining room. He leaned over as far as possible and spotted the outline of an older man hiding behind an antique China cabinet, dressed head to toe in khaki, with binoculars around his neck and a walkie-talkie hooked on his belt.

Fergal turned to Anakin.

"Hey."

"What?"

He nodded his head toward the dining room. "Who's that?"

Anakin looked over his shoulder for a moment and then turned back. He shrugged.

"I dunno. He's been there for three days. I thought he was with you."

"With me?" asked Fergal.

"Yeah, I thought maybe he was a relative. Like a long-lost uncle whom you shunned as a muscular and athletic all-American ideal symbolizing male oppression, sexism, and misogyny."

Fergal stared at Anakin for a moment.

"No."

"Oh," said Anakin. "Well then I don't know who he is."

The man in khaki leaned forward to hear their conversation. He unhooked his walkie-talkie and depressed the button on the side.

"This is Trainor. I've been spotted," he said. "Move in."

The apartment's front door suddenly crashed open and two more men dressed just like Trainor entered. Anakin and Fergal stared blankly.

"Um, civilized people *knock*," said Anakin.

"Tag 'em, boys," said Trainor.

The two men moved in quickly and, before either Fergal or Anakin could react, attached bright yellow RFID tags to their ear gauges. They hung there like big, ugly earrings.

"Who are you?" demanded Fergal. "What's going on?"

One of Trainor's men sized up the two boys.

"You sure these two are hipsters?" he asked Trainor with a smirk.

Fergal and Anakin rolled their eyes.

"Really? You're *seriously* asking that question?" said Fergal.

"Oh, of course we must be hipsters. Because everything has to have a label and be pigeonholed in order to be societally relevant."

"Just forget it. You wouldn't understand," said Fergal.

"They sure sound like hipsters to me," said the man.

"Whatever," said Anakin.

"Gentlemen, my name is Bill Trainor, and I am with the United States government," Trainor said, pulling out his badge and ID.

"Pssh. The government," said Anakin.

"What could the government possibly want with us?" asked Fergal.

"Well, in your quest to not be labeled or pigeonholed, you hipsters have pushed yourselves to the brink of extinction. You've been officially placed on the endangered species list," said Trainor.

He gestured at the RFID tags dangling from their earlobes.

"Now that we've got those tags on you to keep track of your movements, we're taking you fellows someplace safe," said Trainor.

"We *are* safe," said Anakin. "Or we were. *God.*"

"Where are you taking us?" asked Fergal.

"To a hipster preserve," Trainor replied.

"A hipster preserve?"

"Oh yes."

"What's a hipster preserve?" asked Anakin.

"It's a special planned community set aside just for you. It's extraordinary. No expense has been spared. There's an indie rock store that only carries vinyl. An American Eagle. An organic cafe. A thrift store. You'll be among your own kind."

Fergal and Anakin exchanged a glance.

"What about ...?" Anakin prompted.

"Yes?"

Anakin managed to squeeze his hands into his pockets and looked down at his shoes. "Females," he said, mostly to the floor.

"Well of course! You need to multiply, don't you? Propagate the species?"

"Really?" asked Anakin. "What are they like?"

"Well, from what I've seen, they're culturally vapid sorority-type girls with bottled blonde hair, overly tanned skin, and an affinity for whatever sugary pop song is currently most popular."

Fergal and Anakin looked at one another, stricken. Trainor maintained a stone face for as long as he was able, and then burst out in hearty laughter.

"Oh, lighten up, boys! I'm joking! I know those are all symbols of female insecurity, low self-esteem, and lack of cultural intelligence and independent thinking."

Fergal grabbed his heart with his open hand as Anakin let

out a long, slow breath. They looked at one another, smiling.

"When do we leave?" asked Fergal.

"Five minutes," said Trainor. "You'd better get packing."

The hipster preserve was everything Trainor had promised and more. On a bright, sunny morning, Fergal and Anakin sat at an outdoor cafe, the sidewalks bustling with fellow hipsters, and somewhere music played that was so obscure that no one had ever heard of it.

Fergal took a sip of chai tea and looked around.

"Hey," said Fergal.

"What?"

"I think I'd rather be endangered."

"I know, right?" said Anakin. "This place is *so* ten minutes ago."

VIII. TROUBLE BRUIN

"I am. So. Bored," Biggun sighed, staring out the front window of the house he shared with his sister and younger brother.

"Can you stop saying that?" snapped Muff, his sister. "I'm getting really bored with it."

"And I'm getting bored with you being bored with him being bored," said Tiny, their brother. "So I'm three times as bored as he is."

The three of them sat in silence for a while, listening to the sound of the wind whipping through the trees and the rain lashing the windows.

"Hey," said Biggun after a while. "Look at that."

"What?" asked Tiny.

"It's Red," Biggun said thoughtfully, still staring out the window. "Looks like she's headed to her grandmother's."

"She couldn't wait for nicer weather than this?" Muff said.

"Maybe we should invite her in," Tiny said suddenly, his

energy returning. "You know, get her in here, disembowel her, rip her limbs off, chew on her face. The usual drill."

"Hm," grunted Biggun. "It *would* alleviate the boredom."

"We're not eating Red today, so forget it," Muff said, getting up from her chair and walking toward the kitchen. "We have porridge left over from last night."

"Uck," Tiny grimaced. "Porridge is so *boring*."

Muff smacked the back of his head as she passed. "You want to make more exciting food, you be my guest."

"I wanted to eat Red!" Tiny said crossly. "That would have been more exciting!"

"Doesn't matter now anyway," Biggun sighed. "She's gone."

"Aw," Tiny said.

"You can eat your porridge in a violent and horrifying manner if you like," Muff chided. "But you'll have to clean it up."

"Forget it," Tiny grumbled. "I'll eat the stupid porridge in the regular old *boring* way."

"Your bravery in the face of adversity is an inspiration to us all," Muff smiled.

As they made their way into the kitchen, Tiny pulled out the largest of three chairs set around the kitchen table and was about to sit when he heard Biggun's warning voice: "*Don't.*"

"Seriously?" Tiny said as he stepped away from the chair and angled for the smallest of the three. "We really have to do this *every time?*"

"This is my chair, punk," Biggun said curtly.

"So what, I'm the smallest so I have to sit in the smallest

chair and sleep in the smallest bed? How fair is that?"

"I suppose now you want a California King," Muff said from the stove.

"As a matter of fact, yes, I *would* like a California King," Tiny said brightly, dropping down into his small chair. "Or at least a queen."

"And where are we supposed to put it?" Biggun said. "We've only got the one bedroom."

"Well maybe we should start looking for a bigger place," Tiny replied. "It's a buyer's market, y'know."

"Apparently," Muff said to Biggun as she began ladling out the porridge into three bowls, "banks and mortgage lenders have started accepting honey as currency."

"Well that's wonderful," Biggun said, smiling. "In that case, let's find the biggest, most luxurious house in town. We've got plenty for a down payment."

"All right, all right," Tiny said, frowning. "You don't have to be jerks about it."

Tiny raised a spoonful of porridge to his mouth and put his lips to it. "Ow!"

"What?" Muff asked sharply.

"This crap is too hot!" Tiny protested. "Oh, and also, it's crap."

Muff whacked Tiny on the side of the head with the ladle. Biggun put his palm over the surface of the porridge in his own bowl.

"Tiny's right," he said. "It is. Too hot, I mean."

Muff pushed her bowl away. "Well," she said, "what do you want to do while it cools?"

"Well," Biggun said, "it's not much of a day for taking a

walk. I guess we could cruise over to the mall for a bit."

"Good idea," said Muff, rising. "I'll drive."

"Shotgun!" cried Tiny.

"*Don't,*" said Biggun menacingly. "That's my seat, punk."

Lox was lost.

The wind whipped her in every direction and she was soaked to the bone as she staggered along what might have been a road or possibly a river, depending on your definition of things.

"Okay, yes," Lox muttered to herself. "Yes, this was a mistake."

In the gathering darkness she spotted a rough rock wall running parallel to the road and made her way to it, using it to keep herself vertical as the wind tried its best to knock her down.

As she took a moment to get her bearings, she spotted a small cottage a short distance away.

"Oh thank God," she whispered. "Please, please, please let someone in there have an iPhone charger."

She staggered and slipped her way to the front door of the house. Even in the gloom of the storm it looked friendly and inviting. Lox rapped on the door.

"Hello?" she called. "Is anyone home? Hello?"

She knocked again, harder, and took a startled step backwards as the door swung open on its own. Lox didn't hesitate; she immediately dove inside and slammed the storm behind her.

The quiet of the little house was shocking after the maelstrom she'd been wandering in. She peeled off her dripping cloak and hung it on the coat rack nearby.

"Hello? Anybody here?" she called out again. "I'm sorry to barge in, but the door was unlocked. And it sucks out there."

No answer. Just the steady *tick-tick-tick* of a grandfather clock in the corner of the living room.

"Kay. Well. I'll just warm up and dry off a bit," she said, half to herself and half to anyone who might be too shy to answer. "And then I'll be on my way."

She looked around. To her left was an enormous overstuffed leather armchair. Behind her was a slightly smaller glider rocker. And to her right was a small wooden padded chair, with an ornate filigree on top.

She made her way to the big chair and hoisted herself up into it.

"Nope," she said immediately. "That'll make my ass bones ache."

She slid down and made her way to the smaller chair. She flopped into it and was almost consumed by the cushions.

"Ah, no," she said. "I'd rather breathe, if it's all the same to you."

She pulled herself out with great difficulty and walked over to the smallest chair. She hesitated for a moment, and then sat.

"Huh," she said, smiling to herself. "Nice."

She pulled off her soggy boots, and then stripped off her soaked stockings and threw them on the coffee table. Then she wrung out her dripping golden hair and twisted it into a haphazard bun.

"Better," she said. Her stomach growled, almost in response.

She rose and walked over to the doorway that led to the kitchen. Once again, there was an enormous chair, a slightly smaller chair, and a little chair gathered around the table. And on the table were three full bowls.

She approached hesitantly. Sitting in strangers' chairs was one thing, but eating their food was something else altogether. Still, no one was home and she was hungry.

She grabbed the nearest bowl and stirred the contents with the spoon. She took a bite and immediately spat it back out.

"Ugh," she said in disgust. "That's crap."

She grabbed the second bowl and took a bite from it.

"Pleah," she said, spitting it out as well. "That's crap too."

She looked at the third bowl for a moment, then shook her head. "Fool me twice, shame on me."

Lox wandered over to another doorway on the other side of the kitchen. It was a bedroom, and once again had the big, medium, small theme, the same as the rest of the house. Lox went to the largest bed and sat on the edge of the mattress.

"Oh Lord," she muttered. "Like a cinder block."

She crossed to the medium-sized bed and pushed down on the mattress. Her arms disappeared up to her elbows.

"Geez," she said. "No lumbar support at all."

On to the third, and smallest, bed. She sat on the edge and sighed contentedly.

"Nice," she said, repeating her assessment of the smallest chair. She swung her legs up and lay down.

"Five minutes," she said, and was asleep in an instant.

An hour later, Biggun, Muff, and Tiny returned from their trip.

"I just don't see what's so great about Lululemon," Tiny said, wiping his feet on the mat inside the door as the others did the same. "It just looks like regular workout clothes to me."

"Ah, but it isn't," Muff retorted. "It's unbelievably expensive workout clothes."

Biggun made his way straight to his favorite chair and then stopped dead in his tracks. His eyes narrowed and he wheeled on his younger brother.

"Tiny!" he growled.

"What?"

"You've been sitting in my chair!"

"What? No I haven't!" Tiny cried indignantly. "I've been at the mall with you guys! Paranoid much?"

Biggun advanced on him.

"Well someone's been sitting in my chair!" he roared.

"Well that *someone* isn't me!" Tiny shot back. "Geez, what a grouch!"

Tiny stormed off into the kitchen and then disappeared into the bedroom. He came back a few seconds later, a baffled expression on his face.

"What?" asked Muff.

Tiny remained silent, but gestured for the other two to follow him. The three of them entered the bedroom, where a softly snoring Lox lay sprawled in Tiny's bed.

"Tiny!" hissed Biggun. "You know the rules! You're supposed to put a necktie on the door knob!"

"I wasn't in here *with her*, you big dope!" Tiny hissed back. He gave Lox a long, assessing glance and grinned. "Although …"

Muff swatted him hard on the side of the head.

"Who is she?" she whispered. "What is she doing in this house?"

"Maybe she's a thief," Tiny offered up.

"No," Biggun replied. "Thieves are in and out. They don't stick around to snooze."

"A squatter?" Muff asked.

"She doesn't look like a hippie to me," Tiny said.

"Well, whoever she is, nap time is over," Biggun said. "I say we do what we did with that Van Winkle guy last year."

Muff and Tiny smiled.

"Awesome," Tiny said, and crossed over to the side of the bed. Biggun moved to a position across from him, and Muff moved to the foot.

Tiny leaned over and started gently licking Lox's face. Still asleep, she smiled at the sensation, then giggled. She yawned, stretched, and opened her eyes.

Biggun, Muff, and Tiny roared at her at the top of their lungs, fangs and claws bared.

Lox didn't even have time to scream. Her heart stopped from fright and she died in an instant.

"Nice one!" Tiny cried, and he high-fived his brother and sister.

Later that evening, the three bears sat around the table, laughing and dining on a feast.

"Did you see how big her eyes got?" roared Biggun.

Tiny grabbed Lox's eyeballs from the serving platter on the table and held them up in front of his own. "Aaaaahhhhh!" he screamed in mock fright.

Muff pounded the table with laughter.

"Pass me another drumstick, will you Tiny?" Biggun said, wiping tears of laughter from his face.

"Surely," Tiny said. He reached over, grabbed one of Lox's blackened legs, and wrenched it out of its socket. As he did, a charred wallet plopped on the table.

"We cooked her wallet!" Muff said. She grabbed it and thumbed through it until she found an ID. "Her name was Lox."

"Lox?" Tiny repeated.

"Yes, Lox," Muff said thoughtfully. "Huh."

"What?" said Biggun, taking a big bite of Lox's thigh.

"We should have served her on bagels," Muff replied, and the three of them howled with renewed laughter that echoed through the woods.

IX. ROYALLY SCREWED

Ewan checked his reflection one last time to make sure his uniform was crisp, clean, and in every other way presentable.

After all, it wasn't every day one was summoned to Buckingham Palace.

He placed his constabulary helmet squarely on his head, adjusted the angle down slightly, and nodded. Time he was getting on.

He entered the street on an unseasonably bright, sunny London day. The sidewalks were bustling with activity as people from all walks of life made their way here and there. Ewan squared his shoulders, turned on his heel, and marched purposefully toward Trafalgar Square.

As he made his way along, he couldn't help but notice how many young people there were, talking and laughing in small groups, perusing the quaint little shops, and nodding and smiling at one another.

Not that Ewan was much older than they were—he'd be

twenty-four in January—but they were so different that they might as well have been another species. The girls wore embarrassingly short skirts and dresses with bright floral prints; the men wore suits in colors so bright as to make the eyes water. Their hair was long and it seemed they had all agreed that the look of the day was to be mustaches and muttonchop sideburns. Ewan wondered what the Chief Inspector would make of him if he showed up one day, unshaven and unkempt, wearing a canary yellow blazer and trousers. He couldn't disguise the grin that crept onto his face at the thought of it.

Well, it was the Year of Our Lord 1972, and things were changing. Things would most assuredly be changing for Ewan once he reached the home of the Royal Family. But as he had no idea why he'd been summoned, the extent to which his life would change remained, for the moment, a mystery.

He turned right onto The Mall and there, centered off in the distance between rows of trees and gently swaying Union Jacks, was his destination. The excitement he'd felt since waking turned suddenly and unexpectedly to dread. What was he doing? Why did they want him? What if he did something stupid that brought unendurable embarrassment not only onto himself, but on all of London law enforcement?

The palace grew steadily larger as he approached, and he used this last bit of time to go over everything he'd been told. *Bow at the waist. The first greeting is "Your Majesty," and then "ma'am" or "sir." Don't initiate a handshake. If they initiate, no gripping or pumping. No hugging or kissing. No questions of a personal nature.*

By the time he approached the palace gates, he'd broken into a light sweat, but repeating his instructions had made him feel better. Then all of his calm and confidence shattered when he spotted what was waiting in front of the gates: the Captain of the Queen's Guard, an older, weathered gentleman resplendent in his bright red tailcoats and gleaming medals, flanked on either side by a regiment of palace guards, standing rigidly and staring blankly, their bearskins secured tightly to their square jaws.

Ewan stopped in his tracks. Surely this couldn't all be for *him*, could it? He resisted an impulse to turn around and sprint back down The Mall, and, marshaling all the control he could muster, put one foot in front of the other until he found himself standing in front of the captain. He snapped his right hand up in a smart salute, palm forward.

"Sergeant Ewan Hoozarmi, reporting as requested, sir!"

The captain returned his salute, and Ewan lowered his arm, securing it tightly at his side.

"Sergeant Hoozarmi," the captain said. He had a deep, cultured voice, and though he didn't speak loudly, each word carried the weight of authority. "Welcome to Buckingham Palace. Would you follow me, please?"

Ewan saluted sharply again. "Yes sir!"

The gates swung open and the captain turned and passed through them. The rest of the guard quarter-turned right, quarter-turned right again, and followed in formation. Ewan attempted to match their stride, and as the gates closed behind him, one thought flashed across his mind like a streaking comet: *This is really happening.*

A short time later, Ewan found himself seated in the most opulent office he'd ever seen in his life. The rug was a deep shade of red, and matched the magnificent wallpaper in color, if not pattern. There were four massive crystal chandeliers hanging from the ceiling, and the wall he faced was covered from wainscoting to crown moulding with a portrait of a British army officer atop a muscular, rearing horse. Even the chair he sat in, which faced a monstrous oak desk, was lined with velvet and stuffed with what felt like genuine goose down.

The door opened and two men entered: the Captain of the Guard, and another officer Ewan had neither seen nor yet met. The other officer was younger than the captain but older than Ewan, and carried a scowl on his face that could curdle milk. Ewan immediately snapped to attention, but the captain waved it off as he took his own seat behind the desk.

"At ease, Sergeant, at ease. Please, be seated."

Ewan sat back down. The other officer stood rigidly behind and to the left of the captain, his arms locked behind him.

"Sergeant Hoozarmi, may I present my second-in-command, Lieutenant Hollister," the captain said, gesturing to the other officer. In the newly relaxed atmosphere, Ewan forgot himself. He nodded toward Hollister and said simply, "Lieutenant."

It happened in an instant. One moment they were simply three men having a pleasant conversation; the next, it sounded like the office was filled with an air raid siren from the war.

"When you address me, you will stand and salute and call me sir!"

Hollister bellowed so loudly that Ewan's helmet, which had been balanced on his lap, tumbled to the floor. *"Is that clear, Sergeant Hoozarmi?"*

Ewan scrambled to collect his helmet, jumped up, and saluted at once. "Yes sir!"

The captain smiled as he said, "Well, now that's established, you may once again be seated, Sergeant."

"Yes sir!" Ewan saluted again. He was completely rattled as he regained his seat and kicked himself for letting his decorum slip. So much for first impressions.

"Now then," the captain said, drawing up a quill and an inkpot, "I would like to ask you a few questions."

Ewan was still gathering his wits, but in the brief pause that followed, the room once again rang with Hollister's voice. *"When the Captain of the Guard addresses you, you will respond with yes sir or no sir! Is that clear, Sergeant Hoozarmi?"*

"Yes sir!" Ewan blurted out hastily.

The captain continued as if there had been no interruption. "You are currently assigned to a special division of the City of London Police Force, is that correct?"

Out of the corner of his eye, Ewan could see Hollister taking in a deep breath, so he answered quickly, "Yes, sir."

"And what division would that be, Sergeant?"

"Her Majesty's Royal Typo Brigade, sir," Ewan replied.

The captain turned slightly in his chair and exchanged a glance with Hollister, whose expression was unreadable.

"And what is the function of Her Majesty's Royal Typo Brigade, Sergeant?"

"To protect the public from any and all harm arising from typographical errors. Sir."

"I see," the captain said, replacing his quill and leaning back, steepling his fingers under his chin. "So typographical errors—or typos, as it were—are dangerous then?"

"Yes sir," Ewan said. "For ninety-eight percent of the population, they're lethal. Or can be, at least."

"And the other two percent of the population," the captain said, the skepticism clear in his voice now, "join Her Majesty's Royal Typo Brigade?"

"Most do, sir," Ewan said. "But there are also positions available within the government. Office positions and such."

A blanketing silence filled the room, and Ewan sensed what was coming. It would be no surprise. He dealt with it on an almost daily basis.

"Sergeant Hoozarmi," the captain said, standing and placing his arms behind his back, "I'm going to be perfectly frank with you. I think typos are a myth."

He turned to Lieutenant Hollister. "What do you think, Lieutenant?"

"*I agree, sir!*" Hollister bellowed.

Ewan bristled. This was not the first time someone had stated their disbelief of typos, nor was it the first time that it had been implied that Her Majesty's Royal Typo Brigade was a joke. Buckingham Palace or not, Ewan could feel the old familiar anger boiling up inside him, and was not about to let it go unchallenged.

"Typos are not a myth, *sir*," Ewan said through clenched teeth. "I assure you, they are quite real."

The captain smirked, seeming to enjoy Ewan's irritation. "Perhaps one can find typos under the surface at Loch Ness."

Ewan felt his face heat up.

"Or perhaps," the captain said, clearly enjoying himself now, "the ghost of Anne Boleyn carries them with her as she makes her way around the Tower of London."

Ewan stood up, and both the Captain of the Guard and Lieutenant Hollister watched him in amazement.

"With all due respect, *sirs*," Ewan said tightly, "if neither of you has ever seen a typo, it only speaks to the integrity and professionalism of the department I represent. But if, as you seem to be so certain, typos *are* a myth, then you'll not be requiring my specific set of skills. So I'll just show myself out, shall I?"

Ewan stormed out of the office and into a wide hallway lined with old portraits in gilded frames. He marched in a fury, ignoring the call of the Captain of the Guard behind him to return to the office at once.

Who do they think they are? he thought as he crossed into a grand ballroom with sunlight shining through floor-to-ceiling windows, reflecting off the highly polished floors. *Bring me all the way to Buckingham Palace just to have a go at me.*

He passed through a doorway into a formal dining room, where servants setting the massive table watched him with arched eyebrows.

"Sergeant!" the Captain of the Guard shouted from far behind him. "Get back here!"

Ewan ignored him and kept his brisk pace, passing through another doorway and into another hallway, and then into a lushly appointed study. It began to dawn on him that he was lost in the house where the royal family lived and that the only way out would likely be to return with the Captain of the Guard to his office, but he hadn't quite walked off his anger yet. He passed through the study and turned right, and bumped right into her.

"Oh!" she cried, and Ewan instinctively grabbed hold of the young woman's shoulders to steady her. Then he looked at her face and felt his breath leave his lungs as it had never done before.

She was beautiful. Her long, chestnut hair was drawn back in a tight ponytail, and her eyes were a magnificent shade of the deepest blue. He knew her from somewhere, but his mind couldn't place her, because all he could do was drink in her beauty.

"I'm terribly sorry, miss," he heard himself saying, though it might as well have been coming from a distant shore. "Are you all right?"

"Oh. Yes, I'm fine, thank you," she said, and he saw that she was suddenly gazing back at him with an intensity that made his heart speed up in his chest. It only lasted a moment, but to Ewan, it felt like it carried the entire breadth of time itself.

The spell broke as Ewan heard two distinctive gasps behind him. In a trice, two pairs of hands had him by the arms, pulling at him. It was only then that Ewan realized he had never let go of the young lady's shoulders.

"Sergeant Hoozarmi!" the Captain of the Guard whispered furiously through clenched teeth. "Release her at once!"

He and Lieutenant Hollister pulled Ewan away, and then both bowed at the waist to the young woman. "Your Majesty," they said together.

Oh God, Ewan thought, snapping back to reality. *Oh God.*

They're going to hang me.

"Not at all, not at all," the young woman said, and the words were like musical notes to Ewan's ear. "Who is this fine young officer?"

The captain and lieutenant hesitated, not quite sure how to handle the situation. Then the captain grabbed Ewan by the arm and brought him forward.

"Your grace, this is Sergeant Ewan Hoozarmi of Her Majesty's Royal Typo Brigade," the captain said smoothly.

"Oh!" the woman said brightly, and a wide smile crossed her face. "Is this the young gentleman who's been assigned to protect me?"

"Er, yes, ma'am," the captain said. "We were ... just discussing the details when the Sergeant requested a brief tour. In his exuberance, he got away from us and ... accidentally jostled you. Are you all right?"

"Of course I am," she said dismissively, her eyes fixed on Ewan. "In fact, I daresay I have never been better."

She suddenly extended her hand to Ewan. "I am Anne, Princess Royal of House Windsor."

Ewan stared blankly, trying now to remember all he'd been taught about meeting royals. Nothing came. Was it bow? Kneel? Kiss her hand? Sweep her into his arms and ride off down a beach at sunset on a white horse?

Lieutenant Hollister's open-hand slap to the back of his head told him he'd best do something, so he took her hand softly and said, "Your Megistry," followed by a quick bow and a sincere wish that he could crawl under a rock and die there.

Anne smiled even more broadly as she took back her

hand. "I don't believe I've ever been addressed as 'Your Megistry' before. I rather like it. Well, as I'm certain you gentlemen have much to discuss, I'll leave you to it. Good day."

She continued on down the hallway, and the captain and lieutenant bundled Ewan off the way he'd come.

Back in the captain's office, the tension was as thick as ground fog. Lieutenant Hollister looked as though he would eat Ewan for pudding given half the chance, and the captain's face was stony.

"If you ever pull a stunt like that again," the captain said coldly, "I shall have you drawn and quartered, shot, and beheaded, and *then* I shall make things very unpleasant for you. Is that clear?"

"Yes, sir," Ewan said. He knew how much trouble he'd caused, and what an incident he'd created, but all he could think about was Anne's turquoise eyes.

"Now then, may we continue where we left off?"

"Of course, sir."

"As I stated previously, I don't believe in typos, nor the danger that they supposedly pose," the captain said. "But just because I don't believe in something does not mean that it does not exist."

The captain stood and crossed to the other side of the desk, standing directly in front of Ewan.

"There has been a threat made to the princess's life," he said gravely. "Are you familiar with a character who calls himself the Wordmonger?"

Ewan shook his head. Lieutenant Hollister jumped in

immediately with *"When the Captain of the Guard asks you a question—!"*

"Sod off, you," Ewan cut across him, and Hollister looked as though he'd been slapped. Now that he'd survived his brush with royalty and knew that they needed him, he felt emboldened, and wasn't about to allow himself to be bullied.

The captain turned to Hollister, who seemed coiled and ready to tear Ewan's head off. "Lieutenant, please return to your duties."

Hollister looked murderous, but with one last withering stare at Ewan, turned on his heel and left the room.

The captain turned back to Ewan. "Someone calling himself the Wordmonger has indicated that he will attempt to present a typo to the princess and cause her death."

Ewan let the reality of the captain's words sink in.

"Now whether typos are real is not my concern," the captain continued. "The safety of the Royal Family, however, is. And I must take this threat to the princess as seriously as any other."

"Of course, sir," Ewan said.

"Therefore, effective immediately, you will serve as the princess's personal security guard," the captain said, and Ewan felt his chest filling like a balloon. "You will ensure that no typos ever reach her."

"For how long, sir?" Ewan asked.

"Until we can ascertain the identity of this Wordmonger and apprehend him," the captain said.

"Very good, sir," Ewan said brightly.

"Do you have any immediate questions that I can answer?" the captain asked.

"Actually, yes," Ewan said, pulling out his notebook and pen. "The correspondence that comes into the palace. Is it routinely checked?"

"Yes, of course," the captain said with a touch of condescension. "As we ensure that packages don't contain bombs or other explosive devices, we also open envelopes to inspect them for biological agents, harmful substances, and so forth."

"No, but the letters themselves," Ewan said patiently. "Are they read?"

"Yes," the captain said, "but to this point that has been a low priority. I believe the letters are scanned for threats or disturbing language that might upset the family."

"If everything coming into the palace is read," Ewan said, mostly to himself, "it's likely that you already have some CUNTS on staff."

The captain made a sound of complete outrage. "I beg your pardon!" he choked out.

For a moment, Ewan didn't understand the problem. Then it dawned on him.

"Oh! Sorry, yes. That's an acronym. It stands for Civilian Unit Typo Staff. In essence, those who are unaffected by typos but are not members of Her Majesty's Royal Typo Brigade are CUNTS."

The captain stared at him disapprovingly. "Surely you could have come up with a better acronym than *that*."

"I'm not in charge of the acronyms, sir," Ewan said. "Though now that you mention it, that is rather rude, isn't it?"

"Quite," the captain replied. "I would suggest you not

mention these … members of the Civilian Unit Typo Staff around the royal family."

Ewan jotted this down in his notebook. "Hang on a minute … if all of the incoming correspondence is checked, how do you suppose this Wordmonger is going to get a typo in front of the princess?"

The captain gave Ewan a meaningful look. "We suspect," he said slowly, "that it might be, to use the colloquialism, an inside job."

"You think the Wordmonger is inside the palace?" Ewan asked.

"Yes," the captain said simply. "So you can see our predicament."

"Well yes, I certainly do," Ewan said, flipping his notebook closed and tucking it back in his pocket. "I believe that's all I'll need for now. When do I start?"

The captain smiled tightly. "You already have."

Ewan sat in his suite, staring out the window at the twinkling London skyline, unable to process what was happening.

I'm living in Buckingham Palace, he repeated over and over in his head until the phrase lost all meaning. *I'm living in Buckingham Palace.*

His living quarters were sumptuous, although the decor slanted a bit more feminine than he was comfortable with. Everything was done up in shades of pink—the duvet cover, the wallpaper, the drapes, the chandelier, even the bricks surrounding the fireplace. But the furniture, color aside, was the most comfortable he'd ever known. He absently hoped that they never caught this Wordmonger fellow so that he'd never have to return to his council flat.

Of course, he had another reason for hoping they never caught the Wordmonger, and her chambers were directly across the hallway. After settling in, he'd opened and closed the door several dozen times, hoping that he might catch her either coming or going, but her door remained resolutely shut. Of course, it was two o'clock in the morning. What did he expect?

Unable to sleep for a variety of reasons, Ewan reviewed the list of palace staff that the captain had been kind enough to provide him. He might as well have requested a phone book. There were over a thousand people working just within the palace alone, all with unrestricted access to the more than 700 rooms that Ewan was still trying to wrap his head around. If the Wordmonger was indeed inside the palace walls, he was going to have a hell of a job sussing him out.

He tossed the list onto a nearby table, rubbed his eyes, and looked over at the monstrous four-poster bed that dominated the room. He'd been informed that the princess was a late sleeper, but that he should be ready for her at dawn, so a good night's sleep was definitely in order. As he crossed the room from the chair to the bed, unclipping his tie and unbuttoning his shirt at the neck, he heard a very soft rapping at the door.

"Yes?" he called.

"Sergeant Hoozarmi?" a muffled voice said from the other side. "It's Anne."

He was at the door in a flash and opened it so quickly that the princess threw a startled hand to her mouth and laughed softly.

"Your Highness. Is everything all right?" Ewan asked.

"Oh yes, quite," Anne said, smiling. "It's just that I was having trouble sleeping, what with all this Wordmonger trouble afoot, and I thought I might get to know my personal protector a bit better. And as I saw your light was on, I knocked."

Ewan barely heard her. He was taking in every square inch of her face, watching how her full lips formed the words that were coming out of her mouth, getting lost once again in those deep, deep blue eyes. It was only when he realized that silence had fallen between them that he was spurred to speak.

"Oh. Yes. Well, I'm glad you did," he said. "Would you … care to come in?"

"Thank you very much," she said, hitching up the hem of her dressing gown as she crossed the threshold, revealing fuzzy blue bedroom slippers.

Ewan closed the door behind them and watched as Anne looked around.

"I've always fancied this room," she said. "In fact, I had thought to take it as my own, but discovered very quickly that the morning sunlight streams much too directly in for my tastes. Even with the drapes drawn."

"That's good to know," Ewan said. "I shall have to wear my sleep mask to bed."

She laughed heartily, and he felt his heart take flight.

"So," Anne began, "Sergeant Hoozarmi …"

"Please," he interrupted gently. "Call me Ewan."

"Very well," Anne replied, smiling. "Ewan. How did you come to join Her Majesty's Royal Typo Brigade?"

"Oh, well," Ewan said, "they discovered that I was a candidate when I was still in primary school."

"A candidate?" Anne asked.

"Yes," said Ewan. "You see, when you're young, typos don't affect you. But once you hit puberty, either typos become deadly to you, or you display a tic."

"Tic?"

"Yes, well, that's what they call it," Ewan explained. "It's a non-lethal reaction to typos. Everyone in Her Majesty's Royal Typo Brigade has one."

"How fascinating!" Anne said. "And what is your tic? Would you tell me, please?"

"Oh, um ... you see, we normally don't discuss tics," Ewan said. "Not even with one another. Tics are quite personal. And can be a bit ... embarrassing."

"Oh, please do," Anne said. "I promise to take it to my grave."

Ewan grinned. "Well, far be it for a sergeant in Her Majesty's Royal Typo Brigade to deny a request from a member of the royal family. All right. Whenever I encounter a typo, I laugh."

"Well that doesn't sound so embarrassing to me," Anne said.

"Yes, well, it's the manner in which I laugh," said Ewan.

"Oh?"

"Yes, I'm afraid it's quite different from my normal laugh. It's very ... high-pitched. Some might even say exceedingly high-pitched. It's been compared to the hysterical giggling of a young schoolgirl."

Anne attempted to keep a straight face, but burst out

laughing. After a moment or two, Ewan joined her.

"Oh, I am sorry," Anne said, placing a consoling hand on one of Ewan's and causing his heart to skip a beat. "I don't mean to make fun. I only laugh because that's simply adorable."

"Well, it's certainly better than some tics I've witnessed in my time," Ewan said. "I won't name names, but there's a colleague of mine who sneezes uncontrollably when he comes across a typo. And another who balls up his fist and starts bonking himself on the top of the head in a very specific rhythm. Takes him almost an hour to stop."

Anne laughed again, and they lapsed into a comfortable silence where they merely stared at one another. Ewan had all sorts of crazy thoughts about what he might do versus what he knew he should not do, but before he had a chance to act in any way, Anne stood up.

"Well," she said, straightening out her dressing gown, "I'd best be getting back to my chambers. I have a maid who visits quite early in the morning to lay out my jewelry and clothes, and it wouldn't do to have her find me missing."

Ewan stood as well. "No, we certainly couldn't have that. Well, Your Highness, I very much enjoyed our visit and chat this evening."

"As did I," said Anne. "And if you call me Your Highness once more, I shall surely scream. It's Anne."

"Of course," Ewan said. "My apologies. Just one of many things I'm going to need to get used to around here."

"Oh, I think you're going to fit in just fine, Ewan," she said, crossing to the door. "Of that I have no doubt. And I also have no fear of this Wordmonger, now knowing that I have you to protect me."

"With my life, Anne," Ewan said softly. Anne blushed, opened the door, and let herself out.

Ewan crossed to the bed and sat down on the mattress. It was deeper and more plush than anything he'd ever sat on, and he wondered if he'd be able to pull himself out of it when morning came. He swung his legs up, let his head fall into the pillows, and just as he began to think that the picture-perfect night would keep him awake as he replayed it over and over again in his mind, he was fast asleep.

The next morning came very quickly indeed, and Ewan found that his fears had merit—it took a fair amount of time and struggle to extricate himself from the mattress. He showered, dressed, and was ready for duty at 6 a.m. on the dot, but suspected he would probably not see Anne until much later.

He decided to stand post outside Anne's chambers, and was surprised and delighted to find her coming out of her room just as he was coming out of his.

"Oh. Good morning, Anne," Ewan said brightly. "I trust you slept well?"

"Indeed I did," Anne said. She looked very smart indeed in her riding coattails and breeches. Her helmet was tucked casually under her arm and her riding crop was in her gloved hand. "Will you be joining me for my morning ride?"

"Where you go, I go," Ewan replied, and Anne smiled as she took his crooked arm and they made their way toward the center of the palace.

Over the next few weeks, Ewan learned very quickly what a busy life a princess actually led, and how exhausting it was going to be keeping an eye on her at all times.

After a ride through the countryside, it was breakfast with the royal family (during which Ewan was told in no uncertain terms that he could dine downstairs in the servants' kitchen, regardless of how closely he was to be watching her), then it was off to a charity function, then lunch with some foreign dignitaries, then tea with the royals, then a premiere of a new play in the West End, and a quiet dinner alone in her chambers. And that pace kept up day after day. Fortunately, there had been no attempts to introduce a typo into her world, but Ewan remained vigilant.

Nearly a month later, Ewan found himself standing guard outside Anne's chambers as she took a well-deserved nap. Several people passed by in the tending of their duties, as they frequently did, and Ewan gave them all an acknowledging nod. He assumed the underbutler who approached him was passing by as well, but the portly, jowly man in his crisp tuxedo stopped directly in front of Ewan.

"Sergeant Hoozarmi?" the underbutler asked in a deep, refined voice.

"Yes," Ewan replied.

"You're wanted on the telephone," the underbutler said. "If you'll follow me?"

"Oh, I'm, uh, really not supposed to leave my post," Ewan said.

The underbutler folded his hand across his belly and stared at Ewan impassively.

"I'm her personal security, you see," Ewan said, gesturing toward the closed door.

The underbutler blinked slowly, but remained silent.

"Must remain by her side at all times," Ewan said. When there was still no response from the underbutler, he said, "I'm sorry, who did you say was calling?"

"A Chief Inspector Nillie is asking for you, sergeant," the underbutler said at last. "He conveyed that the matter was urgent."

"The Chief Inspector calling for me?" Ewan said, instinctively straightening his tie and smoothing out his tunic. "All right then, yes, lead the way, please."

The underbutler turned and headed off down the corridor, Ewan close behind him. They passed ornate door after ornate door, portrait after portrait, priceless vase after priceless vase as they made their way along.

They reached a wide, magnificent staircase that Ewan had never seen before, then turned right under an archway carved with cherubs and into a small library. They passed servants here and there, but the journey was awkwardly silent, so Ewan initiated small talk to pass the time.

"I'm sorry, I didn't catch your name."

"It's Wrenchley, sergeant," the underbutler said noncommittally.

They passed through a sitting room, turned down another hallway, and continued on through a parlor lined with trophy cases.

"And what do you do here, Wrenchley?" Ewan asked.

"I am an underbutler, sergeant," Wrenchley replied.

"I see. And what does an underbutler do?" They were

passing through one of the smaller ballrooms, on the way to the west conservatory.

"I take coals to the sitting room, clean the boots, and trim the lamp wicks," Wrenchley began. "I lay the breakfast table, carry in breakfast, wait at breakfast, and remove breakfast. I answer the door after 12 o'clock, deliver notes, lay the luncheon table, take in and wait luncheon, clear the table, and clean the silver. I lay the dinner table, I go out with the carriage in the afternoon, and I attend to fires throughout the day and evening. I prepare the table for tea, clean up after tea, wait at dinner, clear the dinner table, help clean the plates, wash the glasses and silver used at dinner, take in coffee and dessert after dinner, wait in attendance in front hall when dinner guests are leaving, attend to the gentlemen in the smoking room, attend to lighting in the house at dusk, and I go out with the carriage in the evening."

"My word," Ewan said. "And what do you do on your days off?"

"If I ever take one, I shall let you know," Wrenchley said. Ewan chortled at this, but Wrenchley's expression remained fixed.

They turned down a short hallway, and at the end of it was a small phone box, a bit like a church confessional. The receiver rested next to the telephone.

"There you are, sergeant, now if you'll excuse me?" Wrenchley bowed, and made his way back the way they'd come.

Ewan sat down next to the phone and grabbed the receiver. He cleared his throat. "This is Sergeant Hoozarmi," he said. "Is that you, Chief Inspector?"

"Well 'ello there, sergeant," a gravelly voice responded. "'Avin fun wif your new girlfriend, are you?"

"Who is this?" Ewan demanded.

"Oh, I fink you know 'oo I am, sergeant," the voice said. "Folks 'ave taken to callin' me the Wordmonger. I kinda like it. Sounds a bit like someone ol' Sherlock 'Olmes would tussle wif."

Ewan looked around. There was no one in this part of the palace he could flag down. Not that he knew what he'd do if there were.

"All right, you have my attention," Ewan said. "What is it that you want?"

"Oh, I fink you know the answer to that too, sergeant," Wordmonger said, and he chuckled in a sinister way. "I want'a slip a typo to that girlfriend o' yours."

"She's not my *girlfriend*," Ewan said, and he instantly felt foolish, like a boy on a playground defending himself against childish taunting. "She is a member of the royal family under my personal protection, and you won't be getting any typos past me."

"Izzat right?" Wordmonger said. "An' 'ow can you be so sure?"

"Because I am by her side at all times," Ewan said proudly.

"I don' fink that's true," Wordmonger said.

"Well then you've been misinformed."

"Oh yeah?" Wordmonger said, his voice suddenly full of menace. "Well. You're not by 'er side right now. Are you, sergeant?"

A cold cloak of fear suddenly closed around Ewan.

Wordmonger was laughing in his ear and he was already on his feet, sprinting back down the hallway, through the conservatory, past the trophies and through the library, up the staircase, and down the impossibly long corridor until, winded and in the grip of near panic, he wrenched open the door to Anne's chambers without so much as a knock.

When he saw what was within, he stopped dead in his tracks, utterly stunned and completely speechless.

There stood Anne in the middle of the room. A note and an envelope lay at her feet. She was completely naked from head to toe, and her right hand was placed over her heart.

And she was singing *God Save the Queen.*

"God save our gracious Queen
Long live our noble Queen
God save the Queen!"

She was looking at Ewan helplessly.
"Anne?" he began, but she simply continued singing.

"Send her victorious
Happy and glorious
Long to reign over us
God save the Queen!"

"Anne!" Ewan said loudly, and he crossed the threshold into the room.

"O Lord our God arise
Scatter her enemies

And make them fall!
Confound their politics
Frustrate their knavish tricks
On Thee our hopes we fix
God save us all!"

Ewan was flummoxed. He grabbed Anne by her bare shoulders and shook her gently, but she just continued singing.

"Thy choicest gifts in store
On her be pleased to pour
Long may she reign!
May she defend our laws
And ever give us cause
To sing with heart and voice
God save the Queen!"

Ewan looked down at the envelope and note at Anne's feet. He snatched them up. In crudely rendered capital letters, the note read WE ALL ADORE YOU, PRINSESS.

Even as Ewan began to giggle helplessly at the typo, a flash of light went off in his head.

Anne was immune.

She was immune to typos, and singing the national anthem loudly while naked, bizarre at it may be, was her tic.

He wanted to communicate all this to her, but between his helpless giggling and her full-throat singing, there was nothing he could do. So on impulse, he embraced her.

And that's exactly the position they were found in when

the palace royal guard stormed into the room, drawn by all the noise.

"Sergeant Hoozarmi!" the Captain of the Guard roared as he drew his saber. The rest of the guards followed suit. "Unhand her royal highness *this instant!*"

Ewan stepped away from Anne and held his hands up, but could not stop giggling. And still Anne kept singing, her hand over her bare white breast.

"Not in this land alone
But be God's mercies known
From shore to shore!
Lord make the nations see
That men should brothers be
And form one family
The wide world o'er!"

The guards wasted no time swarming over Ewan and driving him out of Anne's chambers and into the hallway, where two of the guards wrenched his arms painfully behind his back and began frog-marching him down the hallway. Gasping for breath, trying desperately to stop giggling, Ewan was able to call out one last time: "*Anne!*" The only response he received was her finishing the final verse.

"From every latent foe
From the assassin's blow
God save the Queen!
O'er her thine arm extend
For Britain's sake defend

Our mother, prince, and friend
God save the Queen!"

Ewan sat in Chief Inspector Nillie's office, his head bowed, his face pink and his eyes puffy. A misshapen purple-and-black bruise reached from his right temple to his chin. A cup of untouched tea steamed in front of him.

The chief inspector entered the office, gave Ewan a quick pat on the shoulder, and moved around to sit at his desk. He was older, and a bit jowly, but there was a kindness and understanding in his face that made every member of Her Majesty's Royal Typo Brigade like and respect him.

"So," the chief inspector said gravely. "Bad business, sergeant. Very bad business."

"Sir, please, let me explain—" Ewan started, but the chief inspector held his hand up for Ewan to stop.

"It's all right m'boy, it's all right," the chief inspector said. "I've read the report and I understand exactly what happened."

"You do?" Ewan said disbelievingly, and an enormous wave of relief washed over him.

"I do," the chief inspector said. "And I don't believe you did anything wrong. Well, maybe you shouldn't have been embracing a member of the royal family while she was starkers and singing, but they were extraordinary circumstances, and you did the best you could under them."

"Thank you, sir," Ewan said. "Thank you for understanding."

The chief inspector nodded.

"So ... what *is* going to happen, sir?"

The chief inspector took a deep breath and leaned forward. "This is a highly unusual situation, sergeant," he said. "We have no precedent for this. And everyone has weighed in on it. The Chief Superintendent of the regular police, the Superintendent of Typo Brigade, the heads of the armed forces, Her Majesty the Queen, everyone. I think even the centre forward for Hereford United has put in his two cents' worth."

Ewan offered a wan smile.

"But I daresay that the most impassioned words on your behalf came from Her Royal Highness, Princess Anne."

Ewan suddenly perked up. "Really?"

"Indeed," the chief inspector continued. "She told the truth of it to anyone who would listen. Of course, you know how it is with people and typos. No one wanted to hear it. Or believe it. But they were swayed nonetheless by what she said."

"Anne," Ewan said to himself, and smiled.

"Well, here's the way of it, sergeant," the chief inspector said, folding his hands in front of him on the desk. "There's to be no criminal charges brought against you."

Ewan blew out a deep breath he wasn't even aware he'd been holding.

"But," the chief inspector went on, "you will suffer loss of rank back to constable. And you're to be transferred."

Ewan was still mulling over the idea of going back to constable so it took a moment for this last bit to sink in.

"I'm sorry, sir," he said. "Did you say transferred?"

"Yes."

"Transferred where?"

The chief inspector hesitated, and Ewan got the sense that this was the part he'd been looking forward to the least.

"The States," the chief inspector said simply.

This caught Ewan so off guard that his mind blanked. He heard himself say, "The States? Which States?"

"The *United* States, sergeant," the chief inspector said patiently.

"I'm ... I'm being *deported?*" Ewan blurted out.

"It's best to think of it as a transfer, sergeant," the chief inspector said. "You'll be joining Typo Squad in Los Palabras, California."

Ewan was speechless.

"I think it's important that you know how fortunate you are to have this favorable an outcome, considering some of the suggestions of what to do with you," the chief inspector said. "Did you know there are still dungeons under Buckingham Palace?"

Ewan studied the chief inspector's face to see if he was kidding. He didn't appear to be.

"Sir?" Ewan asked.

"Yes, sergeant?"

"Could I ... would there be any way for me ... to see Anne again? One last time? Before I leave? Just five minutes?" But the chief inspector was already shaking his head.

"I'm sorry, sergeant, but that's quite out of the question. And were I you, I wouldn't get within a hundred yards of the palace. You're likely to get shot. And only shot, if you're lucky."

"And what of the Wordmonger?" Ewan said suddenly.

"He hasn't yet been caught."

"It's up to us to apprehend him, and we will, I assure you," the chief inspector said. "But if your concern is primarily with the princess, take comfort in knowing that she's safe from any harm he could do her."

"Yes, I suppose she is," Ewan said quietly.

"Well, that's all I have for you, sergeant," the Chief Inspector said, standing up. Ewan stood as well. "I suggest you go home and pack. Your flight leaves on Friday."

"I will, sir," Ewan said.

The Chief Inspector extended his hand. "You've been an exceptional officer, Sergeant Hoozarmi. I'm truly sorry to lose you. But I suspect you'll do quite well in your new assignment."

Ewan shook the Chief Inspector's hand. "Thank you, sir. It's been an honor to serve under you."

The Chief Inspector nodded. "Good luck."

"Thank you, sir," Ewan said. He crossed to the office door and left.

Having turned in his uniform and gear, Ewan felt himself quite adrift in the week leading up to his departure. At first he thought he'd spend the time visiting his favorite shops and pubs for a final browse and a pint, but he discovered that was quite out of the question.

He'd become a celebrity.

The goings-on at Buckingham Palace had always been kept under tight wraps, especially from the press, but someone had said something to somebody, and every time Ewan left his flat, he was mobbed by reporters with cameras and open notebooks, badgering him for a photo and a quote. Thankfully, it did not appear that whomever had spoken out of turn had given any details of what happened, but the press knew *something* had happened and that it involved Ewan, and they were all eager to be the first to know his side of the story.

So it was actually something of a relief when Friday finally came. As he was gathering the last of his possessions and packing them away, he heard a sharp rapping on the front door. Sudden irritation flashed. He was in no mood to be sent off by yet another journalist peppering him with an endless litany of questions. He crossed to the front hall, yanked open the door, and before he even saw who it was, shouted, "Piss off!"

"I beg your pardon?" said the man on the stoop. It was Wrenchley, the underbutler from Buckingham Palace, dressed smartly in his tuxedo, a matching overcoat, and a bowler.

"Oh. Forgive me," Ewan said, feeling foolish. "It's Wrenchley, isn't it?"

Wrenchley nodded his head. "Good day, sergeant."

"Oh, I'm ... no longer a sergeant," Ewan said. "Only a constable. And not for very much longer."

"I see," Wrenchley said. "Well, I have a delivery for you, constable."

He reached into his coat pocket and withdrew a bright pink envelope. He handed it to Ewan, whose name was written across the front in impossibly proper script letters.

Ewan felt a jolt of excitement. He stared at the envelope and completely forgot the underbutler standing right in front of him. After a long pause, Wrenchley cleared his throat.

"Oh. Yes. Well … thank you very much, Wrenchley," Ewan said, extending his hand. The underbutler, taken aback for a moment, reached out and shook it.

"The best of luck to you in your future endeavors," Wrenchley said.

"Thank you."

With a small bow, Wrenchley moved away from the doorway and rejoined the flow of pedestrian traffic on the sidewalk. Ewan closed the door, and then hurried into his sitting room.

His hands were shaking so much that it took him two tries to get the envelope open. A page of stationery, covered front to back in the same perfect lettering as the envelope, fell into his lap. He unfolded it and began to read.

My dearest Ewan,

I trust this letter finds you and finds you well. I've just received word of your impending exile and I felt I needed to tell you a few things before you leave these shores.

First, while my heart aches to know that you'll soon be across the Atlantic Ocean, I am wholeheartedly thankful that your punishment wasn't more severe. The things they discussed! And here I thought that England had left the Middle Ages behind.

Second, please know how much I treasured our time together. My only regret is that it was cut so cruelly short.

Third, I wanted to be the one to tell you directly so that you didn't hear the news elsewhere. I've been betrothed to a lieutenant in the Queen's Dragoon Guards. His name is Mark, and whilst we no doubt make an ideal match, he is certainly not you. I sincerely doubt he would know what to do if he ever found me naked and unable to stop singing at the top of my lungs!

And finally, though I'm sure we can both agree how patently absurd my previously undiscovered tic is, know that it will keep me safe from any and all Wordmongers who seek to do me harm.

Have a safe journey to America, Ewan. And know that part of me goes there with you.

Love,

Anne

P.S. I wish to ensure that you end this letter with a smile on your face, so I close with this: Febuary.

Ewan giggled helplessly at the typo as the tears streamed down his face.

If you enjoyed Ewan's story in "Royally Screwed,"
follow his continuing adventures in
TYPO SQUAD.
Available now!

Visit
www.stephenlomer.com
and sign up for the newsletter
to get all the latest information!

ABOUT THE AUTHOR

Stephen Lomer has been writing books, novellas, short stories, and scripts for nearly a decade, and one or two of them are actually pretty good. A grammar nerd, *Star Trek* fan, and other things that chicks dig, Stephen is the creator, owner, and a regular contributor to the website Television Woodshed. He's a hardcore fan of the Houston Texans, despite living in the Hub of the Universe his whole life, and believes Mark Twain was correct about pretty much everything.

Stephen lives on Boston's North Shore with his wife, Teresa.

45850611R00066

Made in the USA
Middletown, DE
15 July 2017